W9-CSL-688

"I don't know about this," Jake said, suddenly afraid.

He didn't like the way the Moops were looking at them.

"What?" Nog asked.

"You might notice that we're outnumbered."

"Don't think of them as outnumbering us," Nog advised. "Think of them as stock."

"I wonder how they think of us," Jake said as the Moops circled round.

"They think of us as—" Nog stopped when he noticed, as Jake had, that the Moops now surrounded them. Jake and Nog stood back to back.

"Hi, guys," Jake said, and waved in what he hoped was a convincingly friendly manner.

The Moops stepped forward. They did not seem angry, or even evil. Their expressions were entirely unreadable. They were totally alien—their needs, desires, and intentions entirely unknown. They closed in, leaving the boys no escape.

The first Moop suddenly spoke a sharp word. Not even Nog had time to cry out when all at once the Moops leaped at the two boys.

Star Trek: The Next Generation
STARFLEET ACADEMY

#1 Worf's First Adventure
#2 Line of Fire
#3 Survival
#4 Capture the Flag
#5 Atlantis Station
#6 Mystery of the Missing Crew
#7 Secret of the Lizard People
#8 Starfall
#9 Nova Command
#10 Loyalties
#11 Crossfire

Star Trek:
STARFLEET ACADEMY

#1 Crisis on Vulcan
#2 Aftershock
#3 Cadet Kirk

Star Trek: Deep Space Nine

#1 The Star Ghost
#2 Stowaways
#3 Prisoners of Peace
#4 The Pet
#5 Arcade
#6 Field Trip
#7 Gypsy World
#8 Highest Score
#9 Cardassian Imps

Star Trek movie tie-in

Star Trek Generations
Star Trek First Contact

Available from MINSTREL Books

For orders other than by individual consumers, Pocket Books grants a discount on the purchase of **10 or more** copies of single titles for special markets or premium use. For further details, please write to the Vice-President of Special Markets, Pocket Books, 1633 Broadway, New York, NY 10019-6785, 8th Floor.

For information on how individual consumers can place orders, please write to Mail Order Department, Simon & Schuster Inc., 200 Old Tappan Road, Old Tappan, NJ 07675.

CARDASSIAN IMPS

MEL GILDEN

Interior illustrations by
Todd Cameron Hamilton

A
MINSTREL®
BOOK

Published by POCKET BOOKS
New York   London   Toronto   Sydney   Tokyo   Singapore

The sale of this book without its cover is unauthorized. If you purchased this book without a cover, you should be aware that it was reported to the publisher as "unsold and destroyed." Neither the author nor the publisher has received payment for the sale of this "stripped book."

This book is a work of fiction. Names, characters, places and incidents are products of the author's imagination or are used fictitiously. Any resemblance to actual events or locales or persons, living or dead, is entirely coincidental.

A MINSTREL PAPERBACK *Original*

A Minstrel Book published by
POCKET BOOKS, a division of Simon & Schuster Inc.
1230 Avenue of the Americas, New York, NY 10020

Copyright © 1997 Paramount Pictures. All Rights Reserved.

STAR TREK is a Registered Trademark of Paramount Pictures.

A VIACOM COMPANY

This book is published by Pocket Books, a division of Simon & Schuster Inc., under exclusive license from Paramount Pictures.

All rights reserved, including the right to reproduce this book or portions thereof in any form whatsoever. For information address Pocket Books, 1230 Avenue of the Americas, New York, NY 10020

ISBN: 0-671-51116-5

First Minstrel Books printing February 1997

10 9 8 7 6 5 4 3 2 1

A MINSTREL BOOK and colophon are registered trademarks of Simon & Schuster Inc.

Cover art by Alan Gutierrez

Printed in the U.S.A.

For the Gilden Girls—
Julia and Beth,
because they're boldly going just about everywhere

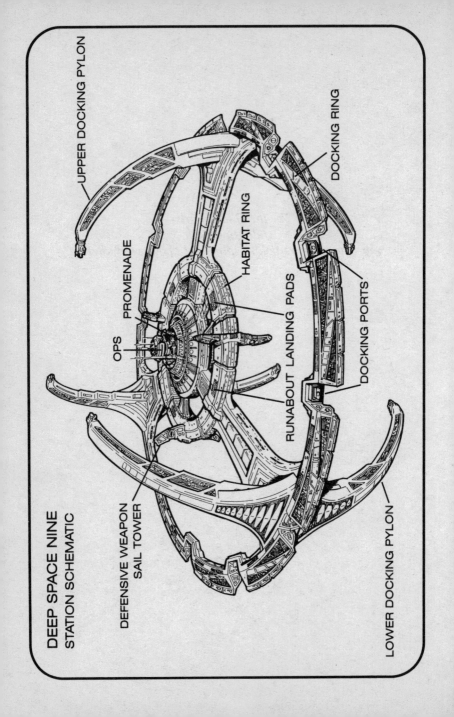

DEEP SPACE NINE
STATION SCHEMATIC

UPPER DOCKING PYLON

DOCKING RING

HABITAT RING

PROMENADE

OPS

RUNABOUT LANDING PADS

DOCKING PORTS

DEFENSIVE WEAPON
SAIL TOWER

LOWER DOCKING PYLON

STAR TREK: DEEP SPACE NINE®

Cast of Characters

JAKE SISKO—Jake is a young teenager and the only human boy permanently on board Deep Space Nine. Jake's mother died when he was very young. He came to the space station with his father but found very few kids his own age. He doesn't remember life on Earth, but he loves baseball and candy bars, and he hates homework. His father doesn't approve of his friendship with Nog.

NOG—He is a Ferengi boy whose primary goal in life—like all Ferengi—is to make money. His father, Rom is frequently away on business, which is fine with Nog. His uncle Quark, keeps an eye on him. Nog thinks humans are odd with their notions of trust and favors and friendship. He doesn't always understand Jake, but since his father forbids him to hang out with the human boy, Nog and Jake are best friends. Nog loves to play tricks on people, but he tries to avoid Odo whenever possible.

COMMANDER BENJAMIN SISKO—Jake's father has been appointed by Starfleet Command to oversee the operations of the space station and act as a liaison between the Federation and Bajor. His wife was killed in a Borg attack, and he is raising Jake by himself. He is a very busy man who always tries to make time for his son.

ODO—The security officer was found by Bajoran scientists years ago, but Odo has no idea where he originally came from. He is a shape-shifter, and thus can assume any shape for a period of time. He normally maintains a vaguely human appearance but every sixteen hours he must revert to his natural liquid state. He has no patience for lawbreakers and less for Ferengi.

MAJOR KIRA NERYS—Kira was a freedom fighter in the Bajoran underground during the Cardassian occupation of Bajor. She now represents Bajoran interests aboard the station and is Sisko's first officer. Her temper is legendary.

LIEUTENANT JADZIA DAX—An old friend of Commander Sisko's, the science officer Dax is actually two joined entities known as the Trill. There is a separate consciousness—a symbiont—in the young female host's body. Sisko knew the symbiont Dax in a previous host, which was a "he."

DR. JULIAN BASHIR—Eager for adventure, Doctor Bashir graduated at the top of his class and requested a deep-space posting. His enthusiasm sometimes gets him into trouble.

MILES O'BRIEN—Formerly the Transporter Chief aboard the *U.S.S. Enterprise,* O'Brien is now Chief of Operations on Deep Space Nine.

KEIKO O'BRIEN—Keiko was a botanist on the *Enterprise,* but she moved to the station with her husband and her young daughter, Molly. Since there is little use for her botany skills on the station, she is the teacher for all of the permanent and traveling students.

QUARK—Nog's uncle and a Ferengi businessman by trade, Quark runs his own combination restaurant/casino/holosuite venue on the Promenade, the central meeting place for much of the activity on the station. Quark has his hand in every deal on board and usually manages to stay just one step ahead of the law—usually in the shape of Odo.

Historian's note: The events of this series take place during the first and second seasons of the *Deep Space Nine* television show.

CARDASSIAN IMPS

CHAPTER 1

Jake and Nog were sitting on the floor of the observation deck, their legs dangling down into the air above *Deep Space Nine*'s Promenade. Behind them were big windows that showed the cold beauty of endless space. Below them, the passing parade of life continued.

A creature twice the size of a human and covered with greenish hair lumbered along the Promenade carrying a tiny silver octopus on its shoulder. Jake thought the small creature was the pet of the larger one until the silver octopus lobbed a small brown chunk to the creature on which it sat, and the larger creature pulled it from the air with a pair of wildly curling tongues. As the big creature chewed, Jake could hear it purr all the way from where he sat.

Something moved so quickly among the creatures strolling the Promenade that Jake did not know if he

was seeing a creature or a machine. Perhaps it was a creature riding a machine.

A crowd of translucent pink domes bobbed by, each trailing strands of goo that quickly evaporated. People avoided the goo and its smell. Jake got a whiff of it himself, and discovered that the smell was pungent and awful.

Four birdlike creatures walked by bearing between them a quivering black ball the size of Jake's head. Was the black ball a life-support canister of some kind, or was it somehow part of the four creatures carrying it?

The runners, the walkers, the squeakers, the bellowers—all these plus the creatures who were more or less humanoid—passed below Jake and Nog. They were not impressed.

"S.O.S." Nog commented.

"Yeah," Jake agreed. "Same old stuff." He could not remember being so bored.

Neither Jake nor his father had wanted to live on DS9, but here they were, and both trying to make the best of it. Commander Sisko had dug in pretty well—he had made friends, and just recently had managed to adjust the replicator in their quarters so that it would make an acceptable version of cayenne pepper.

Jake had made fewer friends, but that was because there were fewer friends to make. The permanent population of children on DS9 was limited—few of the kids who passed through stayed longer than it

3

took to change ships. The only friendship that seemed to have stuck was with Nog, son of Rom, who was the brother of Quark, the Ferengi who owned the most popular bar and restaurant on the station.

Despite his desire to be elsewhere, Jake's first few months on DS9 had been exciting. There was always something new to see or to do. Quark's bar itself had been something of a novelty, offering more exotic delights than were available on many starbases and on all Starfleet ships.

But gradually, the novelty wore off. Aliens he had not seen before arrived at the station all the time— but an extra head, a compound eye, or an unusual skin color no longer excited him.

"Uncle Quark just got a new holosuite program in," Nog said.

"What is it?"

"It's called 'K'lshi: Klingon House of Terror.'" He watched Jake expectantly.

"It's an adult program, isn't it?"

"You bet."

Jake pondered. He and Nog had been through every family holosuite program on the station. And while some of them were fun—the ones not having to do with fluffy animals and pink clouds—Jake was bored. He wanted a new and wonderful experience.

He was certain that "K'lshi: Klingon House of Terror" was exactly what he was looking for. With a title like that, he would no doubt be required to slash and bash and even get dirty. Still . . .

"I don't know," Jake said.

"You're worried about what your father would say."

"Well, yeah," Jake admitted. Commander Sisko would probably not approve of such a holosuite program, and therefore would not allow them to rent it. And Quark never gave away anything for free.

They might be able to get the entry fee from Rom, Nog's father. But if Commander Sisko found out, things would go hard on Jake.

"Let's give it a shot," Nog insisted. "The worst he can do is say no."

"I guess," Jake said. "At least it'll be something to do."

They ran to the lift that would take them up to Ops, a place that was officially off-limits to civilians. But Jake was the commander's son, and that carried certain privileges. And Nog was the commander's son's best friend, so the privileges sometimes covered him too.

When they arrived, the room was empty but for Dax, who was sitting at her science station watching information scroll past on the screen. Though he knew it was true, Jake found it difficult to believe that a lady as pretty as Dax shared her memories and her body with an intelligent, three-century-old worm.

The two boys didn't exactly sneak past her, but they tried to be quiet so as not to disturb her studies. She didn't even look up.

They climbed the stairs to the commander's office. As they approached the doors, Jake saw his father look up from the PADD he was reading and put down the baseball he was turning in his other hand. He beckoned to them, and the doors slid aside.

"Sorry to bother you, Dad," Jake said.

"That's all right. Starfleet reports make me groggy. What can I do for you boys?"

He looked so preoccupied that Jake almost regretted asking a question he knew would probably present a new problem for his already overworked dad.

"You know how you said we should always be open to new experiences?" Jake asked.

"Absolutely," Sisko said. "How else will you learn?"

"Exactly. Thanks, Dad." He turned to go and dragged Nog with him.

"Hold on, there, Jak-o. What's this all about?"

Jake faced his father again. "We just wanted your permission to have a new experience."

"What kind of new experience?" Sisko asked as he smiled. Jake knew that smile. It was an invitation for him to hang himself with his own words.

"Uncle Quark has a new holosuite program," Nog said.

"Ah," Sisko said. "What is the name of this program?"

Jake knew that Nog had doomed them. Yet he also knew that they would have had to tell Commander Sisko eventually.

"It's kind of educational, actually," Jake said.

"And the name of the program is?"

"K'lshi: Klingon House of Terror."

6

"I see. May I suggest that if you gentlemen are looking for something to do, you find Mr. O'Brien. He can always use a pair of willing hands."

Jake grimaced. He liked Chief O'Brien, but he did not relish the thought of crawling through maintenance tubes for the next few hours.

"Or," Sisko went on, "you could just read a book."

"Thanks for the suggestions, Dad."

"Any time." Sisko picked up his PADD and his baseball and went back to work.

Dax was still reading her screen when the boys walked down the stairs to Ops. They got back into the lift and descended to the Promenade.

"I told you Dad wouldn't go for it," Jake said. He'd never really expected Commander Sisko to believe the educational angle, but that didn't prevent him from being disappointed that "K'lshi: Klingon House of Terror" was beyond his reach.

"The holosuite does not provide the only fun on DS9," Nog said suggestively.

Jake had only a vague idea what Nog had in mind, but he didn't think his father would go for it any more than he'd gone for "K'lshi: Klingon House of Terror."

"Fascinate me," Jake said.

CHAPTER 2

There's always food," Nog said. "I'm pretty hungry. How about you?"

"I guess," Jake said. "But we still don't have any money."

"Do you like squarmash and queeble sticks?"

"Love 'em."

"Then don't worry about money," Nog said. "I have a plan."

"Great," Jake said without confidence. Still, he allowed Nog to lead him into Quark's. Jake sat down at a table with certain misgivings.

"This'll be great," Nog said as he settled next to him. Nog was a Ferengi, and as such, he occasionally made sweeping, enthusiastic statements that had no basis in fact.

Jake felt that this was probably one of those times. "Explain it to me," he said. "How can we buy squarmash and queeble sticks if we don't have any money?" Jake really loved squarmash and queeble sticks. Eating them for free seemed too good to be true. He suspected it *was* too good to be true.

"We use credit," Nog said.

"You mean we'll tell your Uncle Quark that we'll eat now and pay him later?"

"That's right. Customers do it all the time. It's called having a bar tab. Even Uncle Quark does it sometimes when he needs to buy supplies and he's caught a little short of latinum."

"I guess it can't hurt to try," Jake said as Quark himself approached them, easily maneuvering around the crowded tables in a way that reminded Jake of dancing.

"You boys staying out of trouble?" Quark asked in a friendly way.

"Yes, sir," Jake said.

"If you're taking up table space, I assume you want to make a purchase."

"Yes, Uncle Quark. We want two orders of squar-mash and queeble sticks."

"I see. You have money?"

"Not at the moment," Nog said enthusiastically. "We were hoping that you might extend us credit."

Here it comes, Jake thought.

"Credit, hmm?" Quark said, and studied them.

Jake was surprised that Quark was considering Nog's offer.

"Yes, sir," Nog said. "We are about to make a huge profit on a big business deal."

"What big—?" Jake began.

"We are about to sell another crate of self-sealing stem bolts," Nog said with much confidence.

"Stem bolts are continually in demand," Quark noted.

"And these are self-sealing," Nog said proudly.

"All right," Quark said. "It's always a good investment to feed two hungry males." He walked back toward the kitchen.

Jake stared after Quark with astonishment. "How did you do that?" he asked, as if Nog had performed a magic trick.

"I have the Ferengi talent for negotiation."

"This is great," Jake said, anticipating his squarmash and queeble sticks.

While he and Nog waited for their food, customers milled around them, playing Dabo, bellying up to the bar (those creatures who *had* bellies), drinking at tables. The establishment was crowded and noisy.

"Maybe your uncle is in a good mood because business is so good," Jake suggested.

"No way. I have a talent for negotiation."

"Well, I hope you can negotiate us some stem bolts."

" 'Wise men can hear profit in the wind.' "

"Rule of Acquisition?" Jake asked.

"Number twenty-two," Nog replied.

A couple of creatures walked in. Neither of them was any taller than Jake, but both were considerably wider. Bullet-shaped, they had no necks as such; their heads grew directly from their muddy brown bodies without a break or a bend, and they were crowned with a three-jaw mouth that clacked constantly as it worked. They did not seem to be wearing clothes, but were sprinkled with golden dust that fell off them in clouds as they moved. Each of them had three arms— one on each side and one in front, and three legs, with the third leg in back.

"What are they?" Nog asked.

"I have no idea," Jake said. "You think they sprinkle themselves with that gold stuff every morning?"

Nog laughed.

"Maybe they do gold one morning and silver the next," Jake suggested, causing Nog to laugh again.

Nog laughed so hard that Jake became embarrassed. If his father were here, he'd probably remind them that the universe was full of beings, and that each was beautiful in its own eyes. Sisko thought that laughing at a species not encountered before was neither appropriate nor kind.

Quark returned with their steaming plates of squarmash and queeble sticks—a glob of yellow stuff with a handful of brown sticks standing up in it. The glob had the heavy smell of meat and spices that made Jake's mouth water. Nog began to shovel small globs of squarmash into his mouth with the queeble sticks, but Jake held the tip of one queeble stick carefully between his thumb and forefinger.

" 'He who pulls the sword from the stone becomes king of England,' " he intoned, and giving his queeble stick a tug, he pulled it from the squarmash and held it over his head.

"What's that all about?" Nog asked.

"King Arthur. An old Earth legend. He pulled a sword from a stone and became king of England."

"What's England?" Nog asked.

"It's a long story," Jake said as he shook his head. When Nog asked questions like that, Jake knew he was a long way from home.

While they ate, their conversation consisted mainly of comments on how much they liked the food. The new aliens drank and played Dabo while clouds of golden dust billowed around them. Jake caught Quark watching them a few times, but he never approached them.

When Jake and Nog were finished, they sat briefly before their empty plates.

"I feel great," Nog said.

"It's been a good day, all right. That was great."

"Better because it was free," Nog said.

"Credit isn't free," Jake reminded him.

"It's free till you have to pay the bill."

They were still laughing about that when Quark came over to their table. "Enjoy the squarmash and queeble sticks, boys?" he asked.

"It was great, Uncle Quark," Nog said.

"That's fine. Time to pay up."

Nog appeared to be as shocked as Jake felt.

"But we were buying on credit," Nog said.

"Self-sealing stem bolts," Jake said. "Remember?"

"We never discussed how long you could have credit," Quark said. "The bill is due and payable now."

"But we don't have any money," Jake said.

"Oh, I wasn't thinking of money," Quark said.

Jake didn't like the oily sound of Quark's voice, and he found out shortly that he was right to be suspicious. Quark gave them each a broom—old style brooms with neither electronics nor passive suction wave generators—and told them to start sweeping up the gold dust the new arrivals had brought in.

"This isn't fair," Nog said. He held the broom away from his body as if it were a Suvian snapping eel.

13

"Of course it's fair. You owe me for the squarmash and queeble sticks. You have no money. I accept your kind offer to work off the debt with the sweat of your lobes."

"We didn't—" Jake began.

"Or, we could take up the matter with Security Chief Odo."

"No thanks," Jake said. He would rather sweep Quark's floor than have Odo report to his father that he'd participated in a Ferengi deal that had been slightly shady from the beginning.

"Get busy, boys. Those miners are leaving a mess everywhere they go," Quark said, and walked back to the bar.

"We've been cheated," Nog said.

"Not cheated," Jake said. "Just outmaneuvered by an expert."

"Whatever. We can learn a lot from Uncle Quark."

Jake did not comment. The Ferengi idea of what passed for education was much different from the human idea. Argument was futile.

Jake had not been sweeping long when he saw that the job was hopeless. The miners seemed determined to play Dabo as long as the wheel was open, and their supply of golden dust seemed to be inexhaustible. The section of floor he'd just finished sweeping looked as if his broom had never touched it.

"You'd think that even Cardassians could clean the station without actually sweeping with brooms," Nog said.

"If you have plenty of Bajoran slaves around, why not let them sweep with brooms?" Jake replied as he shrugged.

Deep Space Nine had been built by the Cardassians as a mining outpost, and not so long ago it had employed Bajoran slave labor for all jobs thought unsuitable for Cardassians. Sweeping out Quark's place would no doubt have fallen into that category.

Jake continued to sweep, but with decreasing enthusiasm. The results were so discouraging. He didn't mind working off his debt, but he wanted something to show for it, if only a clean floor.

"How are you boys doing?" Quark asked.

"Getting nowhere fast," Jake said.

"Put some ears into it," Quark advised.

"It'll take more than ears, Uncle Quark," Nog said. He finished a stroke with his broom just as more of the fine golden dust settled onto the clean floor. "We'll never catch up."

"I hate to throw them out," Quark said as he glanced at the two offending miners. "They're drinking and losing heavily—my favorite combination." He considered for a moment. "You boys get out of here," he said at last as he collected their brooms. "If anybody asks about the dust, we'll say it's our new decor and charge them extra for it."

Jake and Nog did not wait around for Quark to change his mind but ran out of the bar and onto the Promenade. They walked along, oblivious to the familiar shops.

"That garbage is even out here," Jake said. He pointed at the floor where there was more golden dust, pushed into strange patterns by the constant foot traffic.

"At least we don't have to sweep it," Nog said.

"At least sweeping was something to do."

"Good afternoon, boys."

Garak was leaning in the doorway of his haberdashery smiling pleasantly. In his store, any humanoid being could find clothing for any occasion from a formal dinner party to an expedition to the Bajoran outback.

"Good afternoon," Jake said. Nog nodded. Though he liked Garak, Jake was never sure whether to trust him. Whereas Quark was motivated entirely by greed, Garak, being the only Cardassian on DS9, was suspected of having darker motives, more complex motives, political motives. Garak had never been caught spying, but that might mean only that he was a really good spy.

"I couldn't help overhearing that you boys were looking for something to do," Garak said.

"Anything but sweeping floors," Nog said.

Garak seemed surprised by Nog's suggestion. "Oh, I'm sure I can suggest something more interesting than that." He looked up and down the Promenade. "Have you boys ever been down to level forty-five?"

"I didn't know there was a level forty-five," Jake said.

"Well, then, you boys have a real treat in store," Garak said as he rubbed his hands together.

16

"Why?" Jake asked. "What's down there?"

"I have no idea. But if you've never heard of it, I don't imagine many others have either. All kinds of interesting stuff may be down there."

"I don't know," Jake said.

"Could be quite an opportunity."

"Opportunity?" Nog said.

Jake knew that *opportunity* was a magic word as far as Nog and many other Ferengi were concerned.

"Of course. And just think, Jake, how proud your father would be if you found out something about DS9 that nobody knew before."

"What about profit?" Nog asked.

Garak shrugged. "One never knows," he said as he opened his hands, releasing invisible possibilities into the air.

"What's in it for you?" Nog asked.

"For me?" Garak asked, astonished. "Why, nothing. I'm just trying to help."

"Level forty-five?" Nog said.

"That's right," Garak said.

"Thanks for the tip," Jake said. "Come on, Nog."

The boys ran off, but soon slowed down so they could talk. "What do you think?" Jake asked.

"About what?" If an operation showed any possibility of offering financial gain, Nog would generally dive in without thinking twice. He'd gotten burned a few times as a result.

"Garak's suggestion," Jake said. "He might be sending us into a trap."

"Why would he do that?"

"I don't know. But he's a Cardassian. That may be enough."

"He mentioned profit," Nog reminded him.

"Bait," Jake said.

Nog considered Jake's remark. "Maybe we shouldn't go," Nog conceded worriedly.

"Maybe we should."

"Profit," Nog said, as if weighing the two ideas in his mind. "Danger. Profit. Danger."

"Let's talk to Chief O'Brien," Jake suggested. "He knows more about DS9 than anybody. If he says it's all right to go, we will."

"Chief O'Brien doesn't like Cardassians very much."

Nog was right. Chief O'Brien had had confrontations with Cardassians who were much less friendly than Garak, and those experiences had left their mark.

"Well," Jake said, "then we'll just have to be careful how we ask him."

"Right," Nog said.

They rose from the Promenade up to Ops, where they found everything normal. Dax was still engrossed in something at her science console, and Chief O'Brien was laboring over a tricorder at the engineering table. Major Kira was studying the station situation monitor. She smiled at them and then went back to work. Through the fancy door at the top of the stairs, Jake could see his father sitting behind his desk, still turning his souvenir baseball in one hand and reading a report off a padd.

"Hi, Chief," Jake said. He'd helped O'Brien do a few simple jobs, and felt he could be a little familiar.

"Hello, boys," O'Brien said. He had taken apart the back of the tricorder he held. Now, he stuck a dynamic ion brush inside and a tiny tornado of golden dust flew out of the tricorder's insides.

"What is that stuff?" Jake asked.

"That's what I'd like to know," O'Brien said. "It's everywhere."

"A couple of miners brought it on board," Jake said.

O'Brien stopped what he was doing and stared at Jake. "Really," O'Brien said with some surprise. "How do you know?"

"We saw them down in my Uncle Quark's bar," Nog said.

O'Brien nodded and glanced up at Commander Sisko's office.

"Chief," Jake said, "what do you know about level forty-five?"

O'Brien shrugged. "It's a level like a lot of others, I suppose. I've never been down there. Why?"

"No particular reason," Jake said. "We were just wondering."

"Probably nothing down there but a lot of Cardassian dust," Nog said.

O'Brien shrugged. "But I wouldn't put anything past the Cardassians."

Dax strolled over to the engineering table and looked at them over the back of it. When she smiled at the two boys, Jake and Nog could not help smiling back.

"I think I have some answers for you, Chief," Dax said.

"Already? That was quick."

"The dust is called Keithorpheum. It's a fairly common decorative potting soil on some planets, though it's not used much anymore because it gets in everywhere."

"Tell me about it," O'Brien said sarcastically.

"My data base tells me it's harmless," Dax said, "if that's any consolation."

While Dax and O'Brien discussed the Keithorpheum, Jake and Nog backed away from them and quietly left Ops.

"I'll go home and get a couple of flashlights," Jake said when they reached the lift.

"Great," Nog said. "If not even Chief O'Brien has been down to level forty-five, we might find something really good!"

CHAPTER 3

We're getting some unusual sensor readings from Quark's place," Major Kira said as she joined Dax and O'Brien at the engineering station.

"Keithorpheum," Dax said.

"Oh?"

O'Brien lifted his hand and showed Kira the golden dust that lightly coated it. "Jake tells me that a couple of miners came in covered with the stuff."

"It's supposed to be harmless," Dax said.

"A morgo is harmless too," Kira said, "unless it sits on you. I think the commander should hear about this."

The three of them went up to Commander Sisko's office and were invited inside. They gathered around his desk and told him what was going on.

"Sounds like a housekeeping problem," Sisko said.

"So far," O'Brien agreed. "But even stuff that's

harmless on its own can be dangerous if it gets into the wrong places—our air recirculators for instance."

"Major, have Odo visit Quark and see what he knows about the Keithorpheum."

"Aye, sir," Kira said.

"O'Brien, run a level-1 diagnostic on all systems. See that the Keithorpheum doesn't clog up the operation."

O'Brien nodded and left.

"Dax, I want to know all there is to know about this stuff, especially how to get rid of it."

"Right, Benjamin."

As usual, the Promenade was still crowded. Though for convenience sake, DS9 used the Bajoran day and night, the middle of the night might be day for somebody who had just arrived. Warp lag was a familiar discomfort for those who traveled by starship. And, of course, some races slept during the day and were active only at night.

Odo stood with his arms folded across his chest while he looked in through the doorway of Quark's place, presently rollicking with races from across the galaxy. In the middle of the room Quark's brother Rom was sweeping the floor.

An expression of disgust on his face, Odo moved between groups of noisy customers to the bar.

Ignoring Odo, Quark squirted some blue fluid into a small portable antigravity field. The fluid shuddered like a living thing, but soon settled down into a sphere

23

about the size of a fist. As he and Odo spoke, Quark added fluids of different colors, then stuck a needle into the resulting ball and put a puff of whipped cream at the center.

"Business is good," Odo commented.

"So-so," Quark said without looking at him.

"I guess the Keithorpheum isn't bothering anyone."

"The what?"

"The dust," Odo said. "It's called Keithorpheum."

"If you're so interested in dust," Quark said, looking at him at last, "grab a broom. Rom can't keep up."

"Too bad," Odo said without sorrow. "Maybe the stuff will bury you."

When Quark picked up the antigravity field generator, the colorful ball wobbled a little. "Excuse me," he said. "I have a saloon to run."

"First point out the customers who brought in the Keithorpheum."

"Over there at the Dabo wheel," Quark said as he nodded at the two bullet-shaped aliens. They were covered with golden dust that made small clouds every time they moved. "Arrest them if you want to. They're starting to win."

Odo grunted. He walked to the Dabo wheel and watched the aliens through a few turns of the wheel. Quark was right. Each time the wheel stopped, they won a little more latinum. The dust was everywhere.

"Excuse me, gentlebeings," Odo said.

"What?" one of them said, his voice barely more than a growl. Odo could not tell which of the two

24

bullet creatures spoke. Perhaps it didn't matter. Not every hive species was as belligerent as the Borg.

"I am Odo, the security chief of this station, and I have a few questions to ask you."

One of the creatures made a noise which may have signified amusement.

"I must insist."

"You arrest us?"

"I will arrest you if I must. At the moment, I only request the pleasure of your company."

As one, the aliens picked up their latinum and followed Odo to one of the few empty tables. Odo immediately saw that this attempt at courtesy was pointless. Sitting would be impossible for them because they could not bend.

Odo sighed. "You are Trulgovians, are you not?"

"Trulgovians," one of them agreed. Once again, Odo could not determine which one spoke.

"And your ship?"

"Cl'mntin."

"Please return to the *Cl'mntin* and stay there until you learn a little personal hygiene."

"Huh?"

"You're burying the station in this gold dust, this Keithorpheum." Odo picked up a little of it and rubbed it between his fingers. "Wash it off. If you leave your ship again covered in this dust I will arrest you. Do you understand?"

"We mine Keithorpheum."

"I am delighted for you. Leave it on your ship or face the consequences."

One of the creatures growled in what must have been agreement because they took their latinum and their dust and walked out. Odo alerted his security crew that the Trulgovians were on their way to their ship. He wanted to make sure they arrived without mishap.

Quark wandered over and watched the Trulgovians leave. "Not our usual crisis, is it?" he said.

"Be grateful for small favors," Odo said, and walked out.

Level forty-five was not quite the bottom of the habitat ring, but it was very far away from the places Jake and Nog normally frequented. Even the ride on the turbolift took a long time. It could not have lasted more than a few minutes, but to Jake the journey downward seemed to take hours.

When the turbolift doors hissed open they could smell level forty-five even before they saw it. The air had an unpleasant smell that was old and musty—the smell of long-gone Cardassians.

They peered out of the turbolift. The lights that ran along the walls near the ceiling seemed old and weak, yet they cast shadows of struts and beams that were so dark they seemed to be not shadows at all but solid objects. The puffs of faintly glowing mold that grew everywhere looked like tribble colonies. Here and there stood a piece of abandoned equipment. Deck and bulkhead plates were missing in a few places, revealing cables and conduits and junction boxes.

Not far away something made a rustling noise. What kind of creatures lived down here? And did they like their little boys with or without ketchup?

The turbolift beeped at them, impatient to be about its work. Still, the two boys stayed aboard.

"Maybe this wasn't such a good idea," Nog said.

"It looks haunted, doesn't it?" Jake said.

"Haunted?" Nog whispered. "By what? Cardassian ghosts?"

"There are no such things as ghosts," Jake said, sorry he'd mentioned it. The turbolift beeped again.

"What's that noise?" Nog asked.

"Turbolift?" Jake suggested, hoping to lighten the proceedings.

"If you wish to go somewhere else," the turbolift said, making both boys jump, "please state your destination. Otherwise, please exit the car."

"Look at this," Jake said. He stepped off the car and knelt to investigate something on the floor.

"What?" Nog asked, and stepped into the corridor to join him. With a finality Jake found distressing, the turbolift doors immediately slid shut. "Get it back! Get it back!" Nog cried as he leaped from one foot to the other.

"Before we've had our adventure?" Jake asked, trying to sound brave. "Are you kidding?"

"'K'lshi: Klingon House of Terror' is more my speed," Nog said. "I like an adventure I can turn off if I want to."

28

Jake touched the floor and his finger came away sparkling.

"What is it?" Nog asked despite his fears.

"It's Keithorpheum—the stuff those aliens brought into your uncle's bar."

"The air recirculators must have blown it all over the station by now," Nog said.

"I hope it's as harmless as Dax said," Jake said as he stood up.

"Me too."

They walked slowly down the corridor. The air recirculators continued to hiss down here as they did in busier parts of the station, but otherwise it was silent. Jake missed the footsteps, the gabble of voices, and the electronic noises that generally filled his universe.

"Too quiet," Jake said.

"I prefer quiet to screams of pain," Nog replied. "Listen."

Jake strained, and momentarily envied his friend's enormous ears. "I hear running water," he said with amazement.

"Running? Where? From what?"

"Like in a river," Jake said.

"I never heard of a river on DS9."

Nog was right. In Jake's experience, water appeared where it was needed, created by replicators from seed atoms.

A moment later, in the sweat of discovery, they forgot the mysterious sound.

"Look," Nog said as he approached a big window. "It's a store."

"Yeah," Jake said as he glanced around. "There are a lot of stores. It looks kind of like another Promenade." The window was empty except for dust and a few dead insects that the Starfleet personnel called flies; except that these flies were round and flew using air pressure they compressed inside their own bodies.

"We're not going to find anything down here," Nog said. "Let's go." He hustled down the corridor toward the turbolift.

"Go back if you want to," Jake said as he headed in the other direction, figuring that Nog would follow sooner or later. He stopped at the edge of an impenetrable lake of shadow that spread around a corner. "Come on, Nog, I need your flashlight."

Nog cried out, keening in that peculiar way the Ferengi did when they were in trouble.

Jake ran to him and found Nog tangled in a hank of wires that hung from the ceiling. Nog was fighting with the wires as he shrieked, making matters much worse.

"Nog!" Jake cried. Nog came near punching him in the face a time or two as he thrashed around. "Nog!" Jake cried again, and tried to grab his hands. "They're just wires!"

Nog stopped shrieking, which was a relief, and then he quieted down enough to allow Jake to untangle him. "Why do you get so excited?" Jake asked irritably.

"I thought it was one of those Cardassian ghosts."

"Well, it wasn't. It was only some old wires."

"I see that now. I'm not blind."

Jake saw no point in arguing. "Bring your flashlight over here. I want to show you something."

"And then we'll leave," Nog said.

"Right."

Nog brought his flashlight, and aimed it into the shadow. To their surprise, what Jake had found was not just a lake of shadow, but an actual lake. Bubbling

31

up slowly from its center was black sludge that gave off purple highlights where the flashlight's beam touched it. To one side of the seep was a small creature caught in the sludge, which was apparently as sticky as it looked. As it fought the heavy, gluey stuff, the creature let out a soft, breathy whistle.

"What is it?" Jake asked.

"All I know is what I heard at Quark's. A Dabo girl told a customer that there are a lot of creatures who live down on the abandoned levels that we never see higher up. Let's go." He grabbed Jake's arm with one hand and turned away.

"No," Jake said firmly as he removed Nog's hand. "We have to save it." He looked around desperately for a piece of equipment that might help.

"Why? Given the chance, it would probably eat us."

"We don't know that." Jake found a long piece of pipe. "Come on, Nog. Lend a hand," he said as he dragged it toward the lake. The length of pipe was heavy and hard to manage.

Nog helped Jake maneuver the pipe out over the lake. They held it down where the creature could grab it with its tiny paws. It hung onto the pipe with all six of its legs, and looked at them with three big round eyes that reflected what little light there was.

"He's kind of cute," Jake said.

"So is that razor chipmunk Mrs. O'Brien told us about a few weeks ago."

Chief O'Brien's wife taught school when she could

gather enough students to make even a small class. When only Jake and Nog were available, she tutored them in her home. The razor chipmunk she'd told them about was a soft furry creature no bigger than a house cat. It had large eyes and made a pleasing sound. But when caught by a predator—which it seemed to think was anybody who wasn't another razor chipmunk—sharp spines sprang out of its body. The spines were sharp enough to cut off a hand.

"Let's drop it on the *other* side of the lake," Nog suggested.

"That seems mean. What if it's lonesome?"

"What if it's hungry?"

Still upside down, the creature climbed toward them paw over paw. The closer it got, the less sure Jake was that he wanted to take a chance on the creature's intentions.

"Right," Jake said. Helping a creature was one thing. Being a fool was another. Together, they ran the pipe out to its full length and barely managed to set the creature down on a dry level place. As they pulled the pipe back to their side of the lake, the creature sat down at the far edge and looked at them. A moment later it scurried into the darkness.

"There," Nog said. "You see? It's safe. We're safe."

"I guess," Jake said, still not entirely convinced.

"Well," Nog said and rubbed his hands together, "unless you have a plan for crossing this puddle, I guess we've gone about as far as we can go."

Jake thought Nog sounded pretty happy about the

turn of events. And the truth was, level forty-five seemed much less interesting and required much more work than Garak had led them to believe. If his plan had been to get them out of the way for a while, he'd succeeded. Any other motive made no sense.

"All right," Jake said.

As they walked back to the turbolift, Jake pointed the beam of his flashlight here and there, still hoping that they would find something more interesting than dangling wires, wild animals, and sludge. Nog was shining his flashlight around too.

"Have a look at this, Jake."

Jake joined Nog in front of a store that seemed as empty as all the others.

"Look," Nog said, and used the beam of his flashlight to point out something on the floor just inside the doorway.

"It looks like a doll," Jake said. "A Cardassian doll."

"Females play with dolls," Nog said with contempt.

"We came down here to investigate," Jake said as he entered the store. "Let's investigate." He stood over the toy figure and shined his flashlight at it.

The toy figure was obviously supposed to represent a Cardassian—it had the bumpy, lizardlike skin, and the ropelike muscles and tendons supporting the neck. But it also had four wings, a pair of antennae, and a long snaky tail. In its hands it held a view screen in the shape of the characteristic Cardassian oval. On the view screen, each in its own smaller oval, was a holopicture of an object.

"I've never seen a Cardassian with wings," Nog said.

"Me neither," Jake said.

"What do you think it's doing here?"

Jake had the sense that Nog was asking questions to put off the inevitable moment when they would pick up the toy figure. Nog was obviously distrustful, and Jake had to admit that he was too. Cardassian things were always strange and frequently dangerous. Still, how dangerous could a toy figure be?

"The Cardassians left pretty quick. Maybe they left it by accident." He bent to pick up the toy figure.

"Moop!" the toy figure said when Jake touched it. Jake was so surprised, he almost dropped it.

"Moop?" Nog asked.

"Yeah. It's a Cardassian word meaning moop," Jake explained.

"I don't understand."

"It's just a joke, Nog."

"I'll never understand hu-man humor."

"And I'll never understand the Rules of Acquisition. Look at this."

Jake turned the toy figure around so they could both see the screen. On it was an array of small ovals, each one containing an object. In the upper left-hand corner was something that looked like a fish with a definite Cardassian appearance. It was well-armored, and had little knobs and hooks all over its body; a mean-looking whip grew out of its tail. Next to it was a piece of machinery covered with buttons.

"What's that?" Nog asked.

"Musical instrument?" Jake guessed. "Surveying gear? Who knows?" Jake was fascinated by the air of mystery and danger around the Cardassian toy, if that's what it was. Next to the piece of machinery was a nasty but serviceable-looking dagger. It had heavy serrations and extra blades that stuck out from the handle, reminding Jake of Klingon ceremonial blades he'd seen.

"Quite a toad-sticker," Jake said as he pointed to the dagger. He remembered his father's comment about the Klingon blades.

"Yeah," Nog said, and put out his finger to touch the weapon.

When he did, the lights dimmed, and the constant hum of the air recirculators slowed. "Moop," the toy figure said at the same moment, and the dagger seemed to leap off the screen. The boys shrank back as it clattered to the floor between them. The light returned to its usual intensity as did the sound of the air recirculators.

Nog picked up the dagger and studied it as he turned it over.

"It's not a toy," Jake cried. "It's a replicator."

"A toy replicator," Nog said. "And it replicates *good* stuff. Not like the boring machines up on the Promenade." He seemed fascinated by the dagger, and he poked the point into his thumb to see how sharp it was.

"Careful," Jake said.

"I don't feel a thing," Nog said as he poked himself again and again with increasing vigor.

"Let me see," Jake said. He took the dagger from Nog and tried the experiment himself. He found that wherever it touched him, the blade evaporated. The blade reappeared as he pulled it away from his skin.

"Not much of a weapon," Nog concluded.

"Maybe it's not a real weapon," Jake said. "Maybe it's a toy."

"I don't usually think of Cardassians playing with toys."

"Why not? I hear Cardassian have kids. Kids play with toys."

"It doesn't matter," Nog said. "Not much chance for profit selling toys on a space station where you can't find enough kids to make a baseball team." Under the enthusiastic influence of Jake and Commander Sisko, Nog had developed quite an interest in baseball. "Let's go back."

"Profit isn't everything," Jake said, aware that such pronouncements probably did not impress Nog. Being a Ferengi, Nog had memorized most of the Rules of Acquisition as soon as he could read.

Near the blade on the screen were gobs of stuff that might have been food. Jake was going to touch the picture.

"Are you going to eat it?" Nog asked.

"I don't know," Jake admitted. "I want to see what it smells like first."

"I wouldn't waste my time," Nog advised. "It's not only Cardassian food, it's *fake* Cardassian food."

While Jake was still considering that, Nog took the

Moop toy figure from him and was about to touch the screen again.

"Maybe we shouldn't do this anymore," Jake said.

"Why not?" Nog said, his finger poised over a Cardassian animal similar to the one they'd saved from the sludge.

"Because when that little statue replicated the toy knife, the lights dimmed and the air recirculators slowed down."

"Maybe the Moop toy figure is supposed to do that. Besides, you know that DS9 doesn't run too well at the best of times. Just ask Chief O'Brien." Nog laughed.

"And at the moment," Jake added, "the station is full of that sparkly Keithorpheum." He found that his curiosity about the Moop toy figure overcame his concern about the station.

"Right," Nog said. He seemed to lose interest in the animal because instead of touching it into existence, he touched a circle showing a Cardassian warship. The toy figure went "Moop," and three ships sailed out into the air. The boys put up their arms and ducked as the ships began a dogfight, firing phasers and photon torpedoes at each other. One by one the ships disappeared in balls of flame that gave no heat and left no trace. The winning ship just flew through a bulkhead and was gone.

The boys exclaimed their appreciation. Jake grabbed the toy figure away from Nog and studied the array of small pictures. It was his turn to make

something really good—at least as good as the dog-fighting Cardassian ships.

"Look," Jake said, and pointed to a figure much like the Moop statue itself.

"Touch it quick," Nog cried. "Then we can each have one."

Nog's idea sounded so good that Jake immediately touched the screen.

"Moop," the toy figure said.

The Moop toy figure leaped off the screen. But the thing that now stood before them was no doll-size statue. It was nearly as tall as Nog. It put its hands on its hips and spoke to them.

CHAPTER 4

Commander Sisko was draining the last of his most recent cup of *raktajino* when Major Kira and Chief O'Brien asked to see him. They seemed worried.

"What is it?" Sisko asked as he put the empty cup aside.

"Power output of our fusion reactor is down four percent."

"Is that significant?" Sisko asked.

"Not ordinarily," O'Brien said, "Cardassian feedback loops being what they are. What worries me is that sensors indicate that the power conduits are clogged. The clogging is causing the deficiency, and it's getting worse."

"Clogged with what?" Sisko said.

Kira and O'Brien glanced at each other.

"What?" Sisko said.

"The power conduits seem to be clogged with Keithorpheum," Kira said.

"What? That stuff two of Quark's customers brought in?"

"It would seem so," Kira said, obviously uncomfortable.

"Odo says he sent them back to their ship."

"I suspect," O'Brien explained darkly, "by the time he did that, the damage had already been done."

Sisko frowned into his empty *raktajino* cup. "How did the Keithorpheum get in the power conduits?"

"It's everywhere," O'Brien said. He ran his finger along Sisko's desk and held it up for inspection. His fingertip was covered with golden dust.

Sisko ran his own finger over the desk and stared with growing anger at the dust he picked up. "Are the air recirculators maintaining?"

"So far," O'Brien said. "But I don't know how long that'll be true even with my hyperscrubbers on maximum. The funny part is that they seem to be doing their job."

"How can that be if the filters are still clogged?"

"I don't know," O'Brien said with frustration. "According to sensors, when we scrub away one cubic centimeter of Keithorpheum, two cubic centimeters seem to take its place."

"What about the power conduits? I assume you've tried to clean them too?"

"I have, sir," O'Brien said. "With the same result."

Sisko nodded as he looked past them into the main control center. "What does Dax say?"

"She says Keithorpheum isn't supposed to do that.

The stuff has a simple crystalline structure and is nearly inert."

"Then what the hell is going on?"

Dax ran up the stairs and into Sisko's office. "Power is down another three percent."

"Let's find some answers," Sisko said as he stood up.

Jake was astonished. With wary fascination, he looked from the small statue in his hand to the creature—Jake already thought if it as a Moop—as it walked around the store mumbling to itself. Occasionally, it turned and spoke while it waved its antennae at them. When it got no response, it shrugged and went back to its exploration.

"What's it saying?" Nog asked as he edged out of its way.

"I don't know," Jake said. "I think it's speaking Cardassian."

"It doesn't matter," Nog said excitedly. "This is a great opportunity."

"Opportunity?" Jake asked. "For what?"

"This little guy will make a great servant, a great companion."

"We don't know anything about him—or even if it *is* a him," Jake reminded Nog. The Moop was climbing on some shelves at the back of the store. Jake admired its grace and strength; it might be a formidable enemy if it turned out to be less than friendly. "Even if it wants to be a servant or a companion, it'll have a hard time—it doesn't speak Standard English."

"Rule of Acquisition number sixty-two," Nog quoted. 'The riskier the road, the higher the profit.' Let's do a little experiment."

"Be careful," Jake advised, not liking Nog's suggestion.

"It's simple. Watch." He glanced around, and picked up a small electronic part that had a crystalline tube at each end. "Moop," Nog called to the Moop figure.

The creature looked over his shoulder at them.

"Come on down," Nog coaxed, and patted the side of his leg.

"It's not a dog," Jake reminded him.

"What's a dog?" Nog asked.

The creature fluttered it wings to lower itself gently to floor level. It came toward Nog, making what Jake thought of as questioning noises.

Nog gently lobbed the electronic part in the Moop's direction. The Moop stopped, then easily plucked the flying part out of the air. Nog held up his hands, and the Moop threw it back. When Nog caught it, all three of them laughed. Nog threw it to Jake who threw it to the Moop. Jake felt as if he were in a dream as he played catch with Nog and a creature that had been replicated by a Cardassian toy.

"You see?" Nog said as he caught the electronic part. "He's a great companion! We'll all play baseball together. It'll be terrific advertising for our companion service."

"Baseball?" Jake asked, starting to see the possibilities. He and Nog, and sometimes even his dad, played baseball in a holosuite. As a matter of fact, playing baseball was nearly impossible any other way. It would take eighteen kids to make up the two teams necessary for a game—not counting an umpire and spectators—but there were rarely that many interested parties on the station. "Sure," he said. "If we can get these little guys to play, all we'll need for a game is some equipment and an empty cargo bay."

"Great advertising," Nog said again. "People will come out to the game and see these guys. Everybody will want one!"

Jake was not sure that Moop baseball would be as popular as Nog imagined, but playing a real game of baseball appealed enormously. "There are two of us," he said. "All we really need are sixteen more players."

"Let's get to it," Nog said and reached for the toy figure. "I just hope we can find an empty cargo bay."

"Wait a minute," Jake said. "I want to make my team. You can make yours."

Nog nodded—obviously ready to agree to anything.

Jake touched the Moop icon, and a Moop immediately leaped out of the toy figure. As before, the lights momentarily dimmed and the air recirculators slowed.

"It has wings like the first one," Nog noted, "but it doesn't have antennae or a tail."

"Maybe the toy is broken."

"*I* didn't break it."

The boys watched to see what the two Moops would do together. While the tail of the first one thrashed from side to side, they spoke to each other for a moment. The first one supplemented its conversation with the wiggling of antennae. Suddenly, the second one grabbed the first one and leaped upward. They tumbled through the air, flapping their small wings. After a few seconds, they fell to the ground with a bump and rolled around on the dirty floor.

"Stop them!" Nog cried.

"I don't think they're fighting," Jake said. "I think they're playing."

And sure enough, they soon stopped what they were doing, and sat near each other on the floor. They spoke to each other in their own language—probably Cardassian—and pointed out things of interest including Jake and Nog.

Jake touched the screen again, and another Moop jumped out of the statue. This one was also without antennae and tail. Now that there were three of them, it was easy to see that the original Moop, the one who had the antenna and the tail, was the leader. "See," he said, "they all sit the way he does."

Jake made five more Moops. And though he badly wanted to play baseball, he could not help noticing that the lights were somewhat dimmer than they had been and the air was somewhat more stale than it had been before he started generating his team of Moops.

"Maybe we shouldn't do this," Jake said. "Those Moops are doing something to the station."

"You worry too much," Nog said as he took the original toy figure from Jake. "We'll sell tickets to Moop baseball games, and be rich."

"What if they don't want to play?"

"Why wouldn't they?" Nog asked, confused by the question.

"That's not the point," Jake insisted. "The point is, replicated or not, we don't own them. It's not right for one being to own another."

"What about pets?"

Nog's question stopped Jake for a moment. Pets were common throughout the Federation. What was the difference? "I guess," Jake answered carefully, "it's a matter of intelligence. These Moops seem too bright to be pets."

"All right, Jake. If you insist, we won't force them to play. But they'll want to. I'm sure of it."

"I hope you're right."

The lights continued to dim and the noise of the air recirculators became more labored as Nog made the eight other members of his team. One of the Moops was pawing through a bundle of wire. Others rolled on the floor as the first two had. A few talked with the original Moop—seeming to get information from his antennae as well as from his words—while they contemplated the two boys.

"I don't know about this," Jake said, suddenly afraid. He didn't like the way the Moops were looking at them.

"What?" Nog asked. He held the original toy figure while he stared appreciatively at the members of his team.

"If you don't mind the low light and the stale air, you might notice that we're outnumbered."

"Don't think of them as outnumbering us," Nog advised. "Think of them as stock."

"I wonder how they think of us," Jake said as the Moops circled round.

"They think of us as—" Nog stopped when he

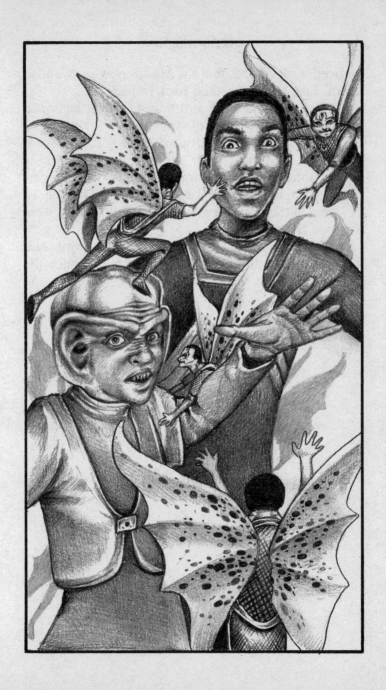

noticed, as Jake had, that the Moops now surrounded them. Jake and Nog stood back to back.

"Hi, guys," Jake said, and waved in what he hoped was a convincingly friendly manner.

The Moops stepped forward. They did not seem angry, or even evil. Their expressions were entirely unreadable. They were totally alien—their needs, desires, and intentions entirely unknown. They closed in, leaving the boys no escape. Jake felt as if he were trapped in a nightmare.

The first Moop suddenly spoke a sharp word. Not even Nog had time to cry out when all at once the Moops leaped at the two boys.

CHAPTER 5

Commander Sisko never did get his lunch.

Once O'Brien had pointed it out to him, he noticed that Keithorpheum covered every surface in Ops. According to sensors and the reports of other personnel on the station, the dust was all over DS9—including, of course, in the air recirculator filters and the power conduits. Everywhere, light, heat, and other life-support services were functioning at lowered levels.

Still, at the moment the Keithorpheum was no more than an annoyance. When questioned about the health risks of prolonged exposure to Keithorpheum, Dr. Bashir looked at the data that Dax provided and pronounced it safe. "Provided," he said, "you don't eat it or become buried in it."

Dax and O'Brien were rigging a way to beam the dust into space. According to Dax, it was just a matter of tuning a wide-angle transporter beam so that it would pick up only the Keithorpheum. The fact that they didn't care in what condition the Keithorpheum arrived at its final destination made matters simpler. O'Brien thought he would have the job done in an hour or two. That left plenty of time before power output fell to dangerous levels.

What irritated Sisko the most was that a pair of Trulgovian miners could bring enough Keithorpheum onto the station to cause trouble. He would not have thought it possible. He suspected something else was going on, and wished he knew what it was.

Therefore, while Dax and O'Brien were seeing to technical matters, and while Kira took care of any further problems the Keithorpheum caused for the station's inhabitants, Sisko and Odo went to visit the miners on their ship, *Cl'mntin.*

The miners had not set foot aboard the station since Odo had warned them to clean up their act, but *Cl'mntin* had not left the docking ring either. The fact that the Trulgovians had stayed at DS9 was unusual, but not exactly suspicious.

"I can't help wondering why they're staying around if they have no intention of visiting the station again," Sisko said as he and Odo marched along the corridor that would take them to the docking ring. The belt pouch in which Odo carried a tricorder slapped against his hip with every step.

"The Trulgovians are not the brightest race in the galaxy," Odo explained. "They make Pakleds look like Daystrom Institute graduates. For all we know, they may still be washing."

"Let's hope that's all they're doing," Sisko said.

The two entered the docking ring, and the big cogged airlock door rolled aside to admit them to the airlock itself. Before them was the meteor-scarred and sun-blasted hull of *Cl'mntin.* Odo worked the intercom and briefly spoke to someone inside the ship. The outer door of the ship slid upward, revealing an interior that surprised Sisko.

Being a Starfleet officer, Benjamin Sisko had seen many different ship designs. The interiors of some ships reminded him of crowded basements or factories. Others seemed more like the lobbies of fancy hotels. Some ignored the emptiness of space while others reveled in it. Each was different. Each suited the needs of the particular race flying the ship. Still, nothing he had seen prepared him for what he saw aboard the Trulgovian ship when he walked in with Odo at his heels.

They stood at the end of a long tunnel that might have been bored right into a mountain. He had heard that the Trulgovians were natural miners, creatures who felt more at home underground than in the artificial corridors of a starship. It seemed they designed their ships to reflect their preference.

Bullet-shaped Trulgovians were trudging single file along this tunnel and through a cross tunnel he saw farther down. Some carried parcels—bags, boxes, or equipment—but they did not speak to each other. As they walked, they kicked up little clouds of golden dust that was certainly Keithorpheum. Sisko supposed that he and Odo would have to undergo decontamination procedures before they reentered the station.

This was all interesting, but not as important as some other facts that Sisko noted.

"The lights are steady," Odo commented, "and taking into account whose ship this is, the air is surprisingly fresh."

"Yes," Sisko agreed. "Apparently, they aren't experiencing the problems with Keithorpheum that we are having."

"Maybe we will find some answers here after all," Odo said.

One of the aliens stepped out of line and approached them. This Trulgovian seemed no different from the hundreds of others in sight. "Come," it said, and walked away without waiting to see what effect its order would have.

Sisko shrugged. "Come," he said, imitating the Trulgovian. As was the custom of the place, he and Odo followed single file.

Following turned out to be more difficult than Sisko had expected. Though a Trulgovian may have been able to tell them apart, all Trulgovians looked pretty much alike to the commander. "Are we following the right one?" he asked Odo.

"I think so, sir. I've been watching our guide pretty closely."

Sisko nodded. He'd been watching too. The fact that he and Odo agreed was a good sign.

They followed the Trulgovian—they hoped it was the right one—up ramps and through enormous caverns where tier after tier of Trulgovians worked, doing things Sisko could not imagine. This was not a real mountain, after all. What could they be digging for?

They made so many turns, went up and down so many tunnels that Sisko was quite lost. He hoped that he wouldn't need to find his own way out.

They came at last to a room where Trulgovians stood among heaps of rock, some of which pulsed with color or glowed steadily. There were no chairs, of course, since Trulgovians did not sit, but a few of the aliens leaned in slanted troughs. Sisko supposed they were comfortable, though they did not look it.

One of the resting Trulgovians turned to Sisko suddenly. "You seek Keithorpheum," it said.

"Not exactly," Sisko said. "We seek a way to get rid of it."

While the Trulgovian thought over that difficult concept, Odo wandered around the room taking tricorder readings. The Trulgovians did not seem to notice.

"We mine Keithorpheum," another Trulgovian said.

"Yes," Sisko said, a little angrily, "and you're leaving it all over my station. You obviously have experience with this substance. How do you prevent it from clogging up your ship's systems?"

Sisko seemed to have stumped them again. He

waited impatiently. His station's air quality and the power output of his fusion reactor were falling as the minutes passed.

"We mine it and we sell it," a Trulgovian across the room explained.

Sisko didn't know whether they were being difficult, or if there was a fundamental difference in the way they perceived language. In either case, he had no time to remedy the situation. "Odo?" he said.

"About done here, Commander." He snapped closed his tricorder and joined Sisko.

"Thank you for your time," Sisko said. "Please show us to the airlock."

None of the Trulgovians moved or said anything.

"Out!" Odo shouted.

One of the Trulgovians walked over to them. "Come," he said, and left the room. Once again struggling to keep the correct Trulgovian in sight, Sisko and Odo set off through the ship. Sisko was pleased and more than a little relieved when they came in sight of the hatch.

They stepped out of the Trulgovian ship and into the airlock, where Odo called a decontamination crew.

"We look like one of them," Odo said as he slapped the Keithorpheum off his clothes. It fell around him in clouds that slowly settled down.

"Yes," Sisko said as he slapped his clothes as well. "Remind me to speak to Dax about her definition of *harmless.*"

The decon crew soon arrived and caused a wave of programmed nanites to wash over them. Each nanite was a microscopic machine that picked up a speck of the dust and carried it to waiting containers. Soon Sisko and Odo and the ground around them was clean.

"Why can't we do that with the station's systems?" Sisko asked.

"Nanites would solve our problem neatly," Odo agreed.

He and Sisko walked back to the habitat ring. Lights were dim and the air was unusually heavy with the musks of metabolizing beings.

"Smells like a locker room," Sisko said.

On the Promenade, the increasingly foul air caused most beings to move slowly, as if they were badly fatigued. A few large-eyed creatures skulked in the growing shadows—night hunters, Sisko was sure. Morose customers sat at the bar in Quark's. Nobody was playing Dabo, so the Dabo girls were, without much enthusiasm, playing some card game among themselves.

"Good luck," Odo said as he handed his tricorder to Sisko. He indicated his office with a nod of his head. "I want to make sure no one is taking unfair advantage of our power reduction."

Sisko walked to the lift, which frustrated him because it rose to Ops so slowly. When he arrived, Dax and O'Brien were standing at the engineering console watching the readout intently. Kira was leaning with both hands on the situation table while she glared at it.

"How are we doing, people?" Sisko asked as he leaped off the lift before it had even risen to floor level. Seeing their faces, he knew he wouldn't like their answers.

"Tuning the transporter for sensitivity to Keithorpheum was no problem," Dax began.

O'Brien, excited, interrupted her. "And as far as we can tell, the transporter is actually picking the stuff up. We've beamed almost a ton of it into space."

A ton sounded like a lot. Not even Trulgovians could toddle around with a ton of dust on their clothes.

"But?" Sisko asked. "I'm sure there's a 'but.' "

"But," Dax went on, "more of it just seems to appear."

"How is that possible?" Sisko said, allowing a little of his anger to show. "You said Keithorpheum was harmless, inert."

"That's what the book says, Benjamin. I'm sorry."

Dax's apology caused Sisko to cool down a little. He knew that Dax and O'Brien were doing their best. His whole team was. He could not help being angry, but acting on his anger was not doing anybody any good. "No need to be sorry," he said. "But I think we must write a new book." He handed Odo's tricorder to O'Brien. "Take a look at these recordings. The Trulgovians can filter out their Keithorpheum. Why can't we?"

"I'll find out," O'Brien said as he took the tricorder and began to download its memory into the station's computer.

"And, O'Brien?" Sisko said.

"Sir?"

"The decon team was able to clean Odo and me up pretty quickly with their nanites. Why can't we just let nanites of that design loose in the station?"

"We could do that, sir, and under ordinary circumstances I would have already suggested it. But if we can't beam the stuff away, I doubt if the nanites would have more luck no matter how fast they ate."

"Understood," Sisko said. "Please carry on."

"He'd better hurry," Major Kira said as she continued to ponder the information on her situation table. "Power output is down another fifteen percent."

As if to emphasize Kira's announcement, gravity fluctuated, and for a moment Sisko felt as if he were on an oceangoing vessel in rough seas. He wished Jake were here where he could keep an eye on him.

"Computer," Sisko called out, "where is Jake Sisko?"

"Jake Sisko is not on *Deep Space Nine,*" the computer said after a moment.

"Please confirm."

"Jake Sisko is not on *Deep Space Nine.*"

"Not possible, Commander," Kira said. "No ships have come in or gone out since yesterday."

"Then something must have happened to his commbadge."

"Possible. I'll get Odo on it."

"Can he spare the officers?"

"I'm sure he can." Kira smiled. "Sometimes you worry too much, Commander."

"Thanks, Major."

Where is that boy?

CHAPTER 6

Terrified, Jake put up his hands to protect himself while Nog keened in distress, a noise that made thinking difficult. The Moops crawled all over Jake, touching him, patting him, lightly scratching him. They pulled his hair and plucked at his clothing, but they did not actually hurt him. They seemed more curious than anything else.

Then one of the Moops ripped off his commbadge and flapped into the air with it. Jake cried out and leaped at the Moop, but it always hovered just out of reach. Nog broke off his keening and tried to help, but had no more luck than Jake.

"Give that back," Jake shouted angrily.

Instead of giving it back, the Moop bit into the commbadge as if to test if it was real. Something inside cracked, and Jake felt a wrenching sickness.

"Now we're really cut off," Jake said, then saw that Nog had troubles of his own.

"Hey," Nog cried as the first Moop grabbed the toy statue and ran to the far corner of the room with it in his hands. While chattering happily to himself, he touched the screen again and again, making more Moops.

The already dim light grew dimmer. The laboring of the air recirculators did little to improve the air quality. The air was also noticeably cooler than normal, and Jake shivered.

Soon the room was filled with Moops, hundreds of them. None of them paid more than passing attention to Jake and Nog.

"Let's warp," Jake whispered, his breath making a plume of mist. He and Nog ran out of the store, and back up the corridor to the turbolift. Jake punched the call button, but the light didn't go on.

Nog set one of his big ears against the closed turbolift door and listened. "I don't think it's working," he said.

The patter of hundreds of feet and the gabble of Moop voices made them look with distress back the way they'd come.

"We can't stay here," Nog cried.

"Come on," Jake said, and ran off, hoping he remembered correctly. He led Nog away from the Moops.

Jake was relieved when he found what he was looking for. He began to undog the hatch cover.

"What is it?" Nog asked.

"Maintenance hatch. Chief O'Brien says they're on every level."

"I guess he was right. Hurry! Hurry!"

Jake didn't have to be prompted. While he fought to make his fingers work correctly on the cold metal, he glanced down the corridor and saw the Moops were already at the turbolift. They would be on them any second.

He got the cover off and dropped it. Secrecy was not necessary. He grabbed the edge of the duct and pulled himself inside. It was full of dust, dead insects, and tiny bits of machined metal. Three of the three-eyed creatures like the one Jake and Nog had saved from the sludge sat to one side staring at him as if with astonishment.

"Come on, come on," Nog cried.

"All right. Just don't get excited," Jake said.

"Excited?" Nog asked irritably as Jake pulled him into the duct. "Why should I be—?" He stopped speaking when he saw the three creatures.

"Come on," Jake cried. "The Moops'll be here any second."

Nog made a small groan of unhappiness as they passed the creatures, squeezing against the far wall as tightly as they could. The creatures turned their heads to watch the two boys, but made no other move.

"I told you they wouldn't hurt us," Jake said as they crawled like mad along the duct. He heard nothing but the mechanical banging of Nog crawling behind him on his hands and knees, and the quick hiss of his own breathing. They crawled for a long time, giving Jake the opportunity to wonder if he should report any of this to his dad, if Garak had known or guessed this would happen, and whether the Moops were following.

For all he knew, Garak's intentions were as innocent as he pretended. Telling his dad seemed like a bad idea, but Jake knew that not telling him was probably worse, especially if the Moops overran the station.

Jake didn't know whether the Moops were chasing them until he stopped at the bottom of a shaft where a couple more of the three-eyed creatures sat waiting.

"Just ignore them," Jake advised as Nog crouched next to him in the tiny space.

A stack of rungs protruded from the wall, making a ladder that converged to a point far above him. The shaft reminded him of the Jeffries tubes—access ways aboard most big starships.

"Yow!" Nog cried.

The Moops were after them, and getting closer very fast.

"Come on," Jake said, and began to climb.

Going hand over hand as quickly as he could, he passed hatchway after hatchway until he lost count; he knew that each hatchway meant he was one level closer to the Promenade. Every time he looked down, Nog was a little farther behind him. A clump of Moops were below Nog, but catching up.

"Come on, Nog!" he cried. Though he knew his life depended on climbing, Jake began to tire and slow down. He would have given anything for a rest. The rungs were so cold that his hands were becoming numb. He didn't think he'd ever be warm again. Then suddenly, cold was forgotten and he was much hotter than he wanted to be. Only by pulling down the sleeves of his pullover to cover his hands was he able to continue climbing the burning rungs. He yelled advice down to Nog.

He grabbed the next rung. When he pulled himself up, he flew upward like a rocket! He automatically put out his hand to grab one of the rungs that rushed past, almost dislocating his arm when he stopped suddenly. A three-eyed creature swam past him, looking very comfortable. It didn't even glance in Jake's direction.

The temperature of the air here seemed fairly normal. But while he looked down, he floated away from the wall as if he were in a pool of water. Apparently, the Keithorpheum was affecting the graviton generators as well as the air recirculators and the lights. Nog seemed far below, and it occurred to Jake that this lack of gravity gave them a chance they might not get again.

"Give yourself a good push," Jake called down the shaft. "We can *fly* up!" The Moops could fly too, of course, but they would leave the zone of regular gravity some seconds behind him and Nog. Jake hoped that a few seconds was all he and Nog would need to get to the Promenade.

Nog shot past Jake, pumping the air with his hands and feet, yelling with delight and fear. Below, the Moops were still climbing hand over hand. Jake gripped a rung and flung himself upward. "Nog!" Jake cried when, a moment later, Nog went past him the wrong way! Jake grabbed him with one hand.

"What happened?" Jake asked. The Moops were shooting toward them.

"Gravity up there," Nog said breathlessly.

Once they entered a zone of gravity, he and Nog would be climbing while the Moops would be flying. Not a good deal. Jake hurriedly shot up to the nearest hatchway and got it open. Beyond was a duct much like the one they had entered far below on level forty-five. After some confusion, Jake got Nog to crawl into the duct first. Then Jake crawled in and dogged it tight behind them.

"That ought to slow them down," Jake said, hoping it was true.

They crawled as fast as they could along the duct. Jake stopped now and then to listen, but he heard nothing but Nog and himself. It seemed too much to hope for that the Moops couldn't figure out how the hatch worked, or had passed the hatch altogether.

After what seemed to be a long crawl, they reached the far end of the duct and Jake had to coach Nog in how to undog the hatch. When the job was done at last, Nog jumped out into the corridor. Jake was right behind him.

The corridor was empty and at least as cold as level forty-five. Lights flickered. Still, Jake recognized this as a residence level, and that made him feel more comfortable. He'd actually been here a few times— once for a birthday party for a little girl who'd gone through the wormhole with her parents the next day.

Jake closed and locked the hatch. He and Nog ran for the nearest turbolift. They ran through another zone of light gravity that allowed them to leap ahead like dancers.

They arrived at the turbolift and Jake stabbed the call button.

"I hear it coming," Nog said, "but it's very slow."

"You want to try the ducts again?"

"If we have to. Let's wait a minute for the turbolift."

They waited impatiently. A moment later they heard a loud bang coming from around the curve of the corridor—certainly the hatch cover striking the floor. The noise was followed immediately by the patter of little feet and loud Moop conversation.

Jake was about to look for another hatch when the turbolift doors slowly opened. He and Nog leaped inside.

"Promenade," Jake cried. He was horrified to see that instead of closing, the doors continued to open until they reached their limit. The boys shouted with alarm when hundreds of Moops boiled into the turbolift with them.

Jake and Nog immediately dashed out, but the Moops did not seem interested in following them. They jostled and climbed over each other as the turbolift doors closed.

When the Moops were gone, Jake and Nog fell on each other laughing with relief.

"Where do you think they're going?" Jake asked.

"Who cares as long as they're gone."

"What if they're going to the Promenade?"

"Their bad luck," Nog said without concern. "They'll have to deal with Odo."

Jake knew that Odo could be tough, but there were an awful lot of Moops. "We're responsible," he said. "We ought to help if we can."

"I guess if we're going to the Promenade too, we don't have a choice."

"Right," Jake said.

Because the Promenade was only a few levels above them, they decided to climb again instead of chancing a ride on the turbolift.

"At the rate that turbolift is moving, we might actually beat them to the Promenade," Nog said.

Whereas the corridor was cold, the duct was surprisingly warm. Gravity in the shaft was higher than it should have been, causing Jake to feel as if he were made of latinum. As they climbed, they passed through a zone where gravity fluctuated so badly Jake felt sick to his stomach. He moved along as fast as he could and soon felt better.

They heard what was going on on the Promenade before they saw it. Angry shouts, the occasional surprised shriek, and Moop-talk echoed back to them along the duct. Cool blue emergency light showed in through the vents of the hatch cover.

"Should we go out there?" Nog asked worriedly.

"Either that or we spend the rest of our lives in this duct."

The prospect seemed to please Nog no more than it pleased Jake. They started to crawl again.

They arrived at the Promenade at last and looked

out of their duct into what seemed to be a brawling crowd. The various types of creatures who inhabited DS9 weren't fighting each other—they were fighting the Moops.

The Moops were climbing over everybody and everything. They grabbed bags, sticks, jewelry, and pieces of equipment and played keep-away with it— throwing things from Moop to Moop over the heads of their victims. They flew through the air with the food and Bajoran ear cuffs they'd collected and peppered the crowd with them. The place was a mess.

"I'm willing to help," Nog said. "Just give me a clue how."

Nearby, a Moop pushed over a booth that usually sold Klingon fast food. The cooking utensils clattered to the floor of the Promenade among a pile of wriggling bloodworms.

Men and women of Odo's security crew dived into the fray, trying to stop the worst of the vandalism, but there were too many Moops, and of course, none of Odo's people could fly. A few of the security team had phasers drawn, but hesitated to fire with so many innocent bystanders around.

"There's Odo!" Nog cried and leaped from the duct into a nest of Moops who poked him and pulled his ears; he struggled against them, alternately laughing and calling out in pain.

Jake leaped down to help his friend, but found that he was just as much at the mercy of the Moops as everyone else. The gravity seemed lighter than normal—perhaps a result of their having been so heavy for so long. The air's temperature was about right, even if it smelled terrible.

Odo was the only one on the Promenade who seemed to be giving the Moops any trouble. Because he could change his shape, the Moops had no target they could prod or pull. Whenever a Moop grabbed him, Odo just wasn't there.

Jake and Nog fought their way free of the Moops and waded through the melee to where Odo shifted from form to form.

"Odo," Nog cried, "we have to tell you—"

"Not now," Odo said with a mouth he formed at the tip of a stalk. "Get to Ops where you'll be reasonably safe. Jake, your father has been very worried."

"Sorry, Odo. But listen—"

Before Jake had a chance to finish his sentence, three Moops got together and carried Odo away. Odo quickly melted between their fingers, took the form of a bird, and flew back to the floor. The Moops who'd grabbed him didn't seem upset by this but dropped to the floor and began to climb Odo like a tree. He melted into the form of a smooth cone resting on its base. The Moops laughed as they attempted to shinny to the top.

"I have an idea," Jake said, and pulled Nog along.

CHAPTER 7

Jake jogged along the Promenade, avoiding the worst of the Moops.

"Where are we going?" Nog cried as he hurried to catch up.

Jake didn't answer, but continued until he arrived at Garak's store. He and Nog stood in the doorway watching Moops try on hats, cloaks, and *katabas* in front of the mirrors. Piles of torn clothing and mashed hats were everywhere, and the displays—normally delicately and neatly arranged—were nothing but a shambles.

Garak ran up and back among the destruction, trying to stop the Moops from doing more damage.

"Hopeless," Nog said.

"You got that right," Jake said. There were too many Moops and not enough Garak to go around.

When he saw the boys, he strode over to them,

picking up pairs of pants and throwing them over his arm as he went. "Things like this didn't happen when I was a child," he complained mildly as he glanced back into his store and sighed.

"Things like what?" Nog asked. "Crazy Moops running rampant?"

"What's a Moop?" Garak asked.

"Those things destroying your store," Jake said.

"Those? Those are Nimijks. I used to own one myself."

"You did?" Jake was confused. "When? Why?" He'd come here because Garak was the only Cardassian on DS9. Not only had Garak sent them to level forty-five, but Jake had assumed that a Cardassian would know more than anyone else on the station about an item found in a Cardassian store. However, with this talk of childhood the discussion had taken an unexpected turn.

"It's quite simple, really," Garak said. Something in his shop crashed, and Garak cringed. "The Nimijk is a Cardassian mythological beast of plenty. Many toy replicators are made in its shape. I had one myself when I was younger." He smiled, remembering. "What I don't understand is why these Nimijks are causing such a commotion. They never did when I was a child." He shook his head.

"It's all your fault," Nog said.

"My fault? The fault of good, simple Garak? Impossible."

"Very possible," Jake said. He and Nog told Garak

how they had found the Nimijk—if that's what it was—on level forty-five, and how the first Nimijk had made more Nimijks, and how all the Nimijks had chased him and Nog back to the Promenade. "And now here they are tearing up the place, and all because you suggested we look around down on level forty-five."

"Suspicious to be sure," Garak admitted. "But the truth is, the power of the Nimijks I owned as a child was severely limited. This sort of disaster would never have been possible." He pursed his lips, thinking.

"You're not a kid anymore," Nog reminded him.

"I don't care about Garak's childhood," Jake said. "The question is, what are we going to do about these Nimijks now?"

"Do?" Garak asked. "Do? Have you tried turning the original Nimijk off?"

"Turning it off?" Jake and Nog asked together with surprise.

"Of course. It's just a toy." A tearing noise in his store caused Garak to briefly grit his teeth. "Where did you say you found it?"

"We told you," Nog said. "In a store down on level forty-five."

"Exactly which store?"

"Are you sure you don't know?" Nog asked accusingly.

"Of course not. You'll have to show me if you want me to help."

"We'll show you," Jake said.

"I'm ready, then," Garak said. He allowed the pants to slip from his arm, and stepped over the heap they made on the floor.

The two boys left the shop with Garak. As they walked along the Promenade among the Nimijks playing in the wreckage of booths, decorations, food, and furniture, Jake thought how strange it was that the survival of *Deep Space Nine* had come to depend on this—the actions of two kids and a Cardassian.

Sisko sat behind his desk, turning his baseball in one hand while he listened to Odo's voice coming over the speaker. "I'm sorry to report it, Commander," Odo said, "but things are getting out of hand down here."

Behind Odo, Sisko could hear the sound of a frightened crowd, things breaking, and security people calling out for calm.

"Any sign of Jake?"

"I saw him on the Promenade—without his commbadge. My guess is one of these creatures took it. In any case, he and Nog both seemed to be fine. I wouldn't worry, Commander. Our little friends seem more interested in property damage than in actually hurting anyone."

"Property damage may be enough," Sisko said, thinking of the plugged up power conduits. He wondered if there was a connection between them and these creatures.

"I suggest you seal off Ops," Odo said. "If these

creatures get control of station systems, there's no telling what sort of harm they can cause."

"Understood, Constable. Keep in touch. Sisko out."

Sisko walked out of his office and stood at the top of the stairs. "Major Kira?"

Kira looked up from the situation table. "Commander?"

"Isolate Ops from the rest of the station. I don't want those creatures in here."

"Aye, sir," Kira said as she began to make adjustments. "And, sir?"

"Yes?"

"Power is down another fourteen percent."

"Thank you for the update," Sisko said, trying to keep sarcasm from his voice. He looked across to the science station. "Anything new?" he asked.

"Actually, yes," Dax said. "I was able to match a picture of one of the creatures with information in the station's original Cardassian data base."

"Those things are Cardassian?"

"In a manner of speaking," Dax explained. "Each of those creatures is in the form of a Nimijk, a mythical creature that is the symbol of abundance in Cardassian folklore."

"All right, then," Sisko said. He felt they were getting somewhere at last. Knowing that his troubles were Cardassian in origin, and did not come from somewhere or something totally alien, gave him a certain comfort. He'd dealt with Cardassians before. He touched his insignia communicator. "Odo?"

A second later, they heard Odo's voice with a lot of crowd noise in the background. "Odo here, Commander."

"See if you can round up Garak and bring him to Ops."

"Garak?" Odo asked, as if he feared that Sisko had lost his mind.

"It's a long story," Sisko said. "Find him as soon as you can. Make it a priority."

"Very well, sir," Odo said, still sounding a little uncertain. "Odo out."

"You think Garak can help us with the Nimijks?" Kira asked.

"*They're* Cardassian," Sisko said. *"He's* Cardassian. I think it's worth a shot."

"Absolutely," Dax said.

Sisko turned to her. "I understand symbols of abundance," he said. "On Earth, the cornucopia fills a similar function. What I don't understand is why a mythical Cardassian creature is destroying my station!"

"Commander?" O'Brien said. He had a worried expression on his face.

"What is it, Chief?" Sisko asked.

"I've been through those tricorder recordings a dozen times." He shook his head.

Dax stared at O'Brien with interest.

"And you found?" Kira said impatiently.

"I found that the Trulgovians' ship is an old D-style freighter—a discount model the Ferengi sell under the name Greased Lightning."

"I've heard stories about D-style freighters," Sisko said, almost smiling. "I understand their failure rate is astonishing."

"Not so astonishing, really," O'Brien said. "Even the Cardassian junk built into this station is better than anything the Trulgovians have. That's why none of this makes sense."

"None of what?" Sisko demanded.

"None of the tricorder readings," O'Brien said, gesturing widely. "I checked Trulgovian life support, their filters, their hyperscrubbers, every cleaning and filtering system on the ship. They are having no trouble at all with the Keithorpheum."

"How are they processing it, Chief?" Dax said.

"The same way they'd process any other impurity in the air," O'Brien said. "That's the hell of it. According to the tricorder readings, their equipment is old, ill-cared for—it was none too good when it was new. It isn't capable of doing anything fancy with the Keithorpheum."

"It must be doing something unusual, Chief," Sisko said.

O'Brien shook his head. "I thought so too. But as far as the Trulgovians are concerned, Dax is right. Keithorpheum is harmless and inert."

Dax and Kira stared at O'Brien. Sisko paced up and back at the top of the stairs. Unexpectedly, a new approach came clear to him. "If what you say is true, Chief, then I suggest we are looking in the wrong place. If the Trulgovians can deal with the Keithorpheum and we can't even though we have better equipment, maybe we're dealing with a different kind of Keithorpheum."

"But the Trulgovians brought the stuff onto the station," Kira said. "It must be the same Keithorpheum they have on their ship."

"Maybe being on the station changed it somehow," O'Brien suggested.

"I'll see what I can find out," Dax said as she began punching codes into her control board.

"Oh, and Dax?" Commander Sisko said, "Check for a connection between these Nimijks and our power problems."

Dax, O'Brien, and Kira looked up at him with surprise, but none of them had a chance to speak before a crowd of small creatures rose quickly out of the shaft through which the lift from the Promenade normally ran.

"Nimijks," Dax cried.

"Don't let them—" Sisko began before he saw that giving such an order was pointless.

The Nimijks quickly spread around the room and leaped onto the situation table. They danced on the science station and on the engineering station, chattering all the while. Lights flashed, gravity fluctuated, and many computer voices spoke at once. Strange chemical smells filled the air. Sisko felt uncomfortably warm.

Disgusted by the chaos he was witnessing, Sisko waded into the thick of the Nimijks and began flinging them off his equipment. Dax, Kira, and O'Brien joined him, but though they labored long and hard, the Nimijks always laughed and came back for more. Sisko saw that he could not hurt them even if he wanted to.

CHAPTER 8

Nimijks were everywhere, throwing and catching random bits torn from the station. In Quark's place they were juggling bottles, much to Quark's dismay. Fragile red bottles, squat green bottles, and jewel-cut orange bottles flew through the air, narrowly avoiding destruction.

"Grab those bottles," Quark called out when he saw Jake, Nog, and Garak, though he himself stood by, not able to do anything but wring his hands.

Jake stepped forward, looking for a way to help, but the Nimijks were too quick for him. Before he'd taken three steps, they allowed all the bottles to smash against the floor. Red liquid, green liquid, and orange liquid splashed and spread. Quark cried out in anguish.

"Excuse us, Uncle Quark," Nog said. "We have to go save the station."

"Go ahead," Quark said as he sank onto a stool. "Desert me in my hour of need."

Farther along the Promenade, in front of Waverly's Wonderful World of Duotronics, Jake, Nog, and Garak stopped and gaped. Jake was not only surprised, but a little charmed by what he saw.

"What are they doing?" Garak asked.

"Playing baseball," Nog said, sounding shocked.

Nog was right. Standing in the open space were two teams of nine Nimijks each. The Nimijks were using a quat—a soft purple fruit—as a ball, and a Lawgiver staff from Beta III as a bat. Jake was horrified by their use of the staff. He had once priced Betan staffs, hoping to give one to his dad as a gift, and he knew how expensive they were.

The Nimijk pitcher wound up and fired the quat at the Nimijk batter, who hit it squarely with the staff, splattering the bright blue pulp all over. All the Nimijks cheered idiotically.

Suddenly, Jake felt guilty. This whole sorry business had started because he and Nog had wanted to play baseball. At the moment baseball didn't seem very important, yet here the Nimijks were, playing it with a fruit and a precious archeological treasure while their friends destroyed *Deep Space Nine*.

"What's the matter, my boy?" Garak asked.

"Nothing," Jake said, wondering again if Garak was even remotely responsible for what was going on.

The turbolifts were still not running, so to return to level forty-five, they had to descend through the maintenance tubes.

"I'm a little old for this sort of thing," Garak said as he eyed the first maintenance duct. "Are you sure this is the only way to get down there?"

"I'm sure," Jake said.

Garak nodded, and gamely, if awkwardly, clambered into the hatchway. He was considerably larger than either Jake or Nog, so it was a tight fit.

At the end of the duct, they entered the vertical shaft and began to descend.

"Light gravity," Garak commented.

"Yeah," Jake said. "Better yet, no Nimijks are after us."

"Not at the moment," Nog said as he looked up.

The shaft above them was empty. As was the shaft below. Apparently, now that the Nimijks had the entire station to play with they had no further interest in Nog and Jake.

The strength of the gravity changed a few times as they descended, once becoming so strong that it seemed to pull their fingers away from the rungs. They needed all their strength to hang on and not plummet to the bottom of the shaft. But through most of the trip the gravity was mild. The temperature changed a few times, first causing Jake to sweat, then causing the sweat to freeze on his body.

"What's that?" Nog asked as he sniffed.

Jake and Garak did the same.

"The air smells rather unpleasant," Garak admitted.

"It's awful," Jake insisted as he made a face. "It's

been getting worse for a while. I hope we can breathe down on level forty-five."

"I'm sure we'll be fine," Garak said.

"How do you know?" Nog asked.

"Oh, I don't know, of course. I'm just trying to maintain a positive outlook."

The air quality got worse, and soon they were all breathing hard.

"I feel as if I'm trying to breathe through a sack," Jake said.

"A sack full of Bajoran dungworms," Nog said.

"That's disgusting," Garak said. "Though I admit," he said after a moment, "that your description is accurate."

They soon came to the duct that would take them out to level forty-five, and crawled along it, breathing hoarsely. When they came to the end Jake and Nog had no trouble jumping out onto the floor, but Garak needed the help of both of them to make it.

A delegation of three-eyed creatures was waiting patiently for them. "Why, what a nice surprise," Garak said when he saw them.

"What are they?" Jake asked.

"Mitz," Garak said. "Cardassian house pets. Some always run away. Some are abandoned." He shook his head. "These must be strays that were left behind when the mining interests left the station."

"We can catch them and sell them," Nog suggested eagerly.

"Not these," Garak said. "These are wild."

"Isn't there anything we can do for them?" Jake asked.

"They seem to be just fine," Garak said. "Where is this store you dragged me down here to see?"

Jake watched the mitz for a moment, wondering if he should come back down here when the station was back under control, and feed them. They were certainly cute, considering that they were Cardassian. "This way," he said at last, and led Garak and Nog down the corridor to the place where they'd found the Nimijk.

Gravity on level forty-five was still light. The air was too cool to be comfortable, and smelled worse than ever. The recirculators ground along, sounding as if they were full of sand. If anything, the corridor seemed dirtier and even more abandoned than it had before. Creatures Jake hoped were only mitz skittered around just out of sight. The light panels that still worked were dim, or flickered—making the movements of the human, the Ferengi, and the Cardassian appear jerky, and giving the whole endeavor a nervous, jumpy feeling.

As they neared the intersection of their corridor and another, a crowd of Nimijks rushed around the corner at them. The Nimijks commented enthusiastically while they danced around them and poked at them and pulled at their clothing.

"What are they saying?" Jake asked desperately.

"I have no idea," Garak said.

"Aren't they speaking Cardassian?"

"Not quite," Garak said as he cocked an ear to listen better. "The Nimijks would understand Cardassian, of course, but among themselves they speak sort of a programming language."

"How'd they know we were coming?" Nog asked as he cringed away from them.

"Maybe they didn't," Garak said. He pushed at the Nimijks a little roughly, but they always came back. "The station is full of Nimijks. I don't find it hard to believe that some would be down here. Do you?"

"I guess not," Jake said, still uncertain about Garak's motives. "Stop that!" he cried as one of the Nimijks reached up to pull his hair.

"Let's do what we came for and get out of here," Nog said.

Jake nodded and continued down the corridor. The Nimijks spread out behind them and followed, still talking among themselves in their programming language. They were nearly at the store where he and Nog had found the Nimijk doll when the Nimijks became quiet and watchful. They were obviously waiting for something. Jake felt fear building inside him. Then something walked out of the shadows.

"It's him," Nog said. "The Moop leader."

"How can you tell?" Garak asked.

"It has feelers and a tail," Jake said. "The others don't."

"Besides," Nog said, "it's carrying the original Moop doll."

The Moop leader waved its feelers, barked a command, and the Nimijks attacked. Their prodding seemed more assertive now; they climbed the three, pulling hair and ears, and poking cheeks. Jake fought them, but it was like fighting a swarm of bugs. No sooner had he brushed a pair of hands away than more hands took their place. Nog started his keen of distress. More and more Nimijks jumped onto Jake's body, and soon their weight forced him to the floor, burying him under what seemed to be hundreds of the creatures.

Garak cried out a single Cardassian word, and a moment later, all the Nimijks were gone—they just disappeared as if someone had switched off a holo-suite program. Nog continued keening.

"Nog," Jake cried as he stood up. "Nog, stop that. We're safe."

"What?" Nog asked as he opened his eyes.

"The Nimijks are gone," Jake said. He picked up the original Nimijk figure from the level, but was careful not to touch any of the pictures on the screen. "The air recirculators sound as if they're moving faster."

"And the lights are brighter too," Nog said.

"May I see that?" Garak asked and held out his hands for the figure.

"After a while, maybe," Jake said. "First, we have a few questions."

"Yeah," Nog said. "A few questions."

* * *

Sisko was on the main floor of Ops, helping where he could. At the moment, he was attempting to keep Nimijks off of Major Kira's situation table so they could get an accurate sense of what was going on in the rest of the station. He lifted Nimijks to the floor and swept them aside, but his efforts went for nothing. More of them always came back.

He tried locking them in his office. This was initially successful because the Nimijks were fascinated by his baseball. But a few escaped every time he opened the door—often more than he had captured. The room had not been designed as a brig.

The Nimijks were a nuisance—always touching things, including Sisko and his staff—but they did not seem eager to do any permanent damage. He'd given up trying to get his baseball back. They weren't hurting it, anyway—just lobbing it around his office.

Sisko still believed there was a connection between the Nimijks and the problem with the Keithorpheum, but so far no one had been able to find it. Part of the puzzle was still missing.

So was Jake, for that matter. No one had seen him since his brief encounter with Odo. Garak seemed to be missing, too. Quark and Rom had been up to complain that Nog was also missing. Jake and Nog had become inseparable, but they did not usually hang around with Garak. Sisko wondered if all three were together. Though DS9 was his first concern, Sisko could not help worrying about his son.

"Commander," Major Kira said, "upper pylon

three reports—" She stopped suddenly, a startled expression on her face.

Sisko had been carrying three more Nimijks up to his office, and was surprised when suddenly his arms were empty. Ops seemed suddenly quiet too, without the gabble of Nimijk voices. Was the light brighter, or was that just his imagination? Fresh, cool air seemed to waft through the big room.

Dax, O'Brien, and Kira were looking at their readouts, dumbfounded. All three began working their boards hard.

"What happened?" Sisko asked.

"I don't know," Kira said as she adjusted controls. "Reports are coming in from all over the station. The Nimijks are gone!"

"Gone where? How?"

"No idea, Benjamin," Dax said as she studied her board. "No residue, no tracks, no traces. It's as if they never were."

"More good news, sir," O'Brien said. "Power output is up seven percent."

"That's great, Chief," Sisko exclaimed. "How did you do it?"

"I didn't." O'Brien sounded confused as he studied his board. "The bad news is, it's not going any higher."

CHAPTER 9

Down on level forty-five, the lights were a little brighter than they had been when Jake and Nog arrived with Garak, and Jake thought he could smell warmer, fresher air now and then. The Nimijks were definitely gone—that was the important thing.

"Why didn't you do that before?" Jake cried with exasperation. He could not help suspecting that the disappearance of the Nimijks was a Cardassian trick, though he had no idea what such a trick might buy Garak or anybody else.

"What? Turn off the Nimijk?" Garak chuckled lightly. "You can't just yell the command into the air. I had to wait till I could speak to the original Nimijk figure."

"I guess that makes sense," Nog said. "Where did they go?"

"Go? Ah, yes." Garak went up to a wall and studied it minutely as he spoke. "I think I told you the Nimijk is only a toy?" He turned to stare at them intently, looking for confirmation.

"Suppose you did," Jake said, trying to remember.

"Well," Garak went on, "because it's a toy, the objects it creates can't hold their matrix after the power supplied by the replicator is turned off."

"I get it," Jake cried. "The statue sort of holds things together. When you turned it off, the Nimijks fell apart into their component atoms. Like pouring water on a sand sculpture at the beach."

"Exactly." Garak seemed pleased.

"What if they come back?" Nog asked worriedly.

"They can't just appear out of the air," Jake assured him. "I don't think they can come back unless we start playing with this Moop statue again."

"Give it to me," Nog said and reached for the toy. "I'll throw it down a recycling chute."

Jake was about to hand over the figure, but he noticed that Garak was watching them with enormous interest. He wished he knew what Garak wanted them to do—and whether he had their best interests at heart. Jake decided to go with his guts. "Not yet," he said. "We might need it."

"For what?"

Jake shook his head. "Don't you think we might need it?" he asked Garak.

"I couldn't say," Garak said, astonished by the question.

Jake had a new thought. "Besides, you originally sent us down here because we might find something new that would interest my dad. I think this is it." He shook the Moop figure at Garak.

"Of course," Garak said, apparently pleased. He frowned and shook his head. "But I still don't understand how the Nimijks got so out of hand. The power of those toys is severely limited. Show me where you found it."

"This way," Nog said and walked down the corridor.

Garak followed him. Despite his fears, Jake could not see the harm in what Nog was doing, so he followed Garak.

Nog led them to the empty shop where they'd found the toy. It was much as they'd left it, though the dust was disturbed, and one of the shelving units had fallen over.

"Looks as if the Nimijks had a party," Jake said.

"Perhaps it was the mitz," Garak said. He glanced at the front window of the shop and laughed out loud.

"What's so funny?" Nog asked, irritated that he didn't know.

"No wonder we had such trouble with that Nimijk!" Garak cried. "This is a repair shop!"

They all laughed, but Jake stopped when he realized that while the nature of the shop explained some things, it did not explain everything. "So, the toy was broken, right?"

"It follows as the night follows the day," Garak said.

"And because it was broken," Jake went on, "the

toy could somehow leach power from the station and use it to make the Nimijks."

"Correct," Garak said proudly. "That is certainly why the figure was taken to the repair shop in the first place."

"Okay, fine," Jake continued. "But if you turned off the figure, why is the gravity still light? Why are the lights still low and the air still bad?"

Garak could not have been more surprised if Jake had thrown a plate of live *gagh* in his face. "I don't know," he said finally. He seemed genuinely bewildered.

"I think we better get this thing to Ops," Jake said. "Dad and the others are going to want to have a look at it."

"I was hoping you would give it to me," Garak said. "For sentimental reasons."

"What's it worth to you?" Nog asked.

Garak laughed again. "You are a Ferengi worth his ears, aren't you, my boy!"

He continued to laugh as they walked back down the corridor. Jake carried the toy, somehow not trusting even Nog with it. Nog might impulsively throw it down a recycling chute. And who knew what Garak might do with it? Jake didn't believe he wanted the figure just for sentimental reasons.

As they passed the turbolift on their way to the maintenance access duct, Jake noticed that the ready light was dim but on. "Let's try this," he said. "Taking the turbolift has to be faster than climbing the maintenance tube again." He pushed the button.

Nog could hear the car in the shaft, but it took so long to arrive that even Garak—an actual adult—seemed impatient. A crowd of mitz gathered around them. The door opened at last, and they entered. Jake found himself to be sorry to leave the mitz behind. He'd have to come back here. "Promenade," he requested. The doors closed, but the car didn't move.

"Let me try," Garak said, and once again barked a word in Cardassian. The car creaked, then began to rise slowly.

"Pretty good," Nog said.

"Oh, Cardassian can be a handy language," Garak admitted.

The ride aboard the turbolift took so long, Jake wondered if climbing the maintenance tube might not have been faster after all. The three of them didn't speak much, though Garak did offer to hold the Nimijk figure if Jake was tired. Jake assured him he was fine.

The ride seemed even slower because Jake was in a hurry to get to Ops. Garak had apparently turned off the figure, and yet there were still some serious things wrong with the station. He, for one, didn't want to spend any more time where he couldn't depend on the power source. Out in space, power meant life. Without power, *Deep Space Nine* was just a useless metal doughnut.

Jake felt a lot older when the turbolift arrived at the Promenade level at last. When they got out of the car, they stepped right into the arms of Odo and a security team.

"Sensors on the turbolift told us you were coming," Odo said, "but we feared you would never arrive."

"Here they are, Odo," Garak said. "Safe and sound." He waved and turned to walk away. "I must go see to my store." A security woman stepped in front of him, and he looked at Odo, stricken. "Surely I'm not under arrest," Garak said. "The boys will tell you I'm quite innocent."

"Innocent of what?" Odo asked.

"Come come, Constable," Garak said. "When the chief of security takes an interest in my activities, I think I am safe in assuming I am under suspicion for *something?*"

Odo smiled as if the effort pained him. "Not under arrest, no," he said with heavy sarcasm. "But I thought that as a concerned citizen of *Deep Space Nine,* you would be delighted to accompany me to Ops and answer Commander Sisko's questions."

"Of course," Garak said. "Delighted. Absolutely."

"Can we come too?" Nog asked.

"I insist on it," Odo said in a way that Jake found troubling.

The lift between the Promenade and Ops was as slow as the turbolift they'd ridden earlier, but the trip was much shorter. Also, the air up here was much better than it had been down on level forty-five— though it was still tinged with the smell of alien sweat. When they arrived, Sisko, Dax, and Kira were standing around O'Brien, who was making adjustments to his engineering board and swearing. Sisko beamed, ran to Jake, and embarrassed him by engulfing him in a big hug.

"Dad," Jake protested halfheartedly.

Commander Sisko backed away, and the smile disappeared as if it had never been. Jake knew that look. It meant the welcome was over and he was in big trouble. He was not sure why he was in trouble, but he was certain it had something to do with level forty-five, the Nimijks, and the station's loss of power.

"Where have you and Nog been, Jake?" Sisko asked.

"Level forty-five."

"What were you doing there?"

"Looking around. We found this," he said as he handed the Nimijk statue to his father.

Sisko turned and showed it to his staff. O'Brien crossed his arms, and Kira looked stern. Even Dax frowned.

"All right, Garak," Commander Sisko said angrily, "let's have it."

"It?" Garak asked. "What?"

"I want you to explain exactly how it happened that creatures looking like this doll badly disrupted the operation of this station."

"It's our fault, Dad," Jake said. "Mine and Nog's."

Sisko turned back to them. "You have my complete attention," he said.

"You see, we found the figure down on level forty-five."

"So you said. But you still haven't explained what you were doing down there. Without permission."

Jake and Nog looked at each other. Jake knew the truth would come out sooner or later, but he didn't want to get Garak in trouble. After all, he hadn't *forced* them to go.

"I suggested they go," Garak said.

"Oh really."

"They were looking for an adventure, and I thought level forty-five would provide a relatively safe one."

"Apparently, you were wrong," Odo said.

"A miscalculation. I am very sorry."

"You don't know sorry," Sisko threatened. "You haven't seen sorry. Go on, Jake. Explain how it's your fault that these Nimijks were all over the station."

Jake could see they were in for it now. There was no avoiding an explanation. "Nog and I found this statue, and it made things. You just touched the screen and it would make Cardassian food or a ceremonial knife—lots of things."

"It was fun," Nog explained. "Want me to show you?"

"Not right now, Nog," Sisko said. "Go on, Jake."

"Then we made these Nimijks. We called them Moops because of the noise the toy made when it worked. And then the first Moop—I mean, Nimijk started to make others. Pretty soon level forty-five was crawling with them."

"They were everywhere," Nog agreed. "We climbed the maintenance tube to get away from them. But they beat us to the Promenade."

"You don't say," Odo commented dryly.

O'Brien seemed puzzled. "Do you think this toy

somehow was able to use station power to make all those Nimijks?"

"The boys found the figure in a repair shop," Garak said. "It was probably taken there for that very reason—it was using station power to make its replications."

"Fine," Sisko said. "That explains the Nimijks. But the power conduits are still clogged with Keithorpheum."

"Power is still down seventy-five percent," Kira confirmed. "With life support at that level, the air will get dirtier and dirtier, and gravity will become more erratic. In less than twelve hours the whole station will just grind to a halt."

CHAPTER 10

Kira's announcement made everybody frown in concentration. Jake and Nog looked around nervously, as if the walls were already closing in.

"It can't be the toy's fault," Nog said. "Garak turned it off." He looked at Jake. "Didn't he?"

O'Brien stepped forward and ran a tricorder over the figure in Sisko's hand. "Dead as a post," O'Brien reported. "But it does contain traces of Keithorpheum."

"I'm not surprised," Kira said. "The stuff is everywhere."

A theory formed in Jake's brain. It all fit! It worked! "Maybe the Keithorpheum infected the figure," he suggested.

Everyone looked at Jake with astonishment. Jake tried to smile. Maybe what he'd just said was stupid.

"That's brilliant, Jake," Dax said. "If the Keithorpheum got into the figure's memory, the figure might have created Keithorpheum the same way it created toys and Nimijks. The Trulgovians didn't bring it all aboard—just the original sample. The rest of it was made by the figure."

"You mean the Keithorpheum clogging our power conduits is not real Keithorpheum but stuff replicated by this toy?" Kira asked. She seemed skeptical.

"Is that possible, Dax?" Sisko said.

"I know very little about Cardassian toys," she said, "but Kira's argument fits the situation."

"Not exactly," Garak said. "As you yourselves have just proven, the figure is—to use Chief O'Brien's colorful phrase, 'dead as a post.' The things the figure produces can't hold their matrix without a constant supply of power. The toy can not possibly be the source of our current problem."

Once more they were stumped. Sisko set down the figure and looked at his senior staff. Jake was glad that he and Nog no longer seemed to be responsible for the crisis aboard the station. Still, according to Dax, he had been brilliant once. Maybe he could do it again.

"Unless . . ." Nog said, and stared at Jake.

"Unless," Jake said, "the replicated Keithorpheum is maintaining its matrix by drawing power directly from the power conduits it is clogging."

"Exactly what I was about to say," Nog said.

"Garak?" Sisko asked.

Garak seemed surprised to be consulted. "I have no idea," he said. "I'm only a simple retailer."

"Perhaps," Odo said.

Kira shook her head. "Replicated Keithorpheum.

No wonder we had trouble getting rid of it, even though our equipment was better than the old stuff the Trulgovians had."

"No wonder," Sisko agreed.

"Jake has a good theory," Dax said with admiration.

"There is a way to find out if it's correct," O'Brien said. He seemed uncomfortable.

"I don't think I'm going to like this," Kira said.

"Probably not," O'Brien agreed. "But it may be our only chance. The only way to stop feeding that Keithorpheum power is to shut down the fusion reactor."

"I'm stunned," Odo commented.

"As am I, my friend," Garak said. He sat down.

"Shutting down the reactor will be a lot of trouble," Kira said. "Getting it up again will be even more."

"We don't have to shut down the reactor," Jake said. "We only have to stop power from flowing through the power conduits."

"In any case," Kira explained, "stopping power to the station will mean shutting down all systems—including life support."

Jake knew how risky Kira's suggestion was. He'd thought earlier about the effect a lack of power might have on the station, and here they were—in such a fix that they were considering doing it to themselves.

"We can survive without life support for a few minutes," Sisko said. "What do you say, Chief?"

"I say that maybe this was what Garak had in mind all along."

"What's that?" Garak said.

"Maybe you knew that toy figure was down on level forty-five. When Jake and Nog were looking for something to do, you saw your chance to unleash it."

"Unleash it?" Garak asked, seemingly horrified.

"You knew what the figure could do, and you trusted the curiosity of a couple of kids to start the ball rolling. What's going to happen once we're shut down? Will your Cardassian buddies fly in and take over again?"

"Come come now, Chief," Garak said. "Isn't that all a bit circumstantial? Even if I planned and plotted as you suggested, how could I possibly have arranged to have those Trulgovian miners arrive at the exact moment Jake and Nog were looking for a project? Even *you* must admit the coincidence is absolutely mind-boggling!"

"I admit nothing," O'Brien said. "You're nothing but a—"

"Chief," Sisko said quietly.

O'Brien looked at him, still fuming.

"Will you answer my question? Can we survive without life-support for a few minutes?"

"I suppose we can."

"Suppose?"

O'Brien took a deep breath and drew himself up. "We can do it, sir. It's just a matter of cross-connecting the power conduits with the emergency power dump, but doing it at the reactor end. We'll shunt everything we have into space."

"How long will that take to set up?"

"Fifteen, twenty minutes."

"If everything is down, how will we get the station back on line?"

O'Brien shrugged. "I'll rig a fail-safe switch. All I'll have to do is release it."

"Very well. You and Dax get on it."

Dax went to stand near O'Brien, who was already making adjustments to his board.

"Major, open the intercom. I want to talk to everybody on the station."

"Right, Commander." She touched her situation table here and there. "Go ahead," she said.

"Attention, please," Commander Sisko said. Jake could hear his voice rumbling through the station. He imagined Quark and all the other merchants on the Promenade listening and fearful; he imagined Mrs. O'Brien and the others who might be at home in the habitat ring gathering up their pets and children, preparing for the unpleasantness to come.

"As you have certainly noticed," Sisko went on, "we are experiencing a power shortage. Our science and engineering staff believes they have found a solution to our problems, but it will require us to shut down all station systems for a brief time. This means *all* station systems, including life-support. All lights will be off, all air recirculators will be non-operational. Gravity and temperature control will be down. This is a drastic measure, and there is some danger involved, but the shutdown will not last long and it is absolutely necessary. We will begin in approximately fifteen minutes. Go to a safe place and stay there until the lights come on again. Thank you for your cooperation."

Jake was really proud of his father. Though Commander Sisko sometimes got excited, he seemed never to be afraid. He was a good man to have around in a crisis; a good man to admire. Maybe he was right about the "K'lshi: Klingon House of Terror" holosuite program. There would be time for it later, if he and Nog were still interested.

Dax and O'Brien continued to work. Quark and Rom came up, and for once Commander Sisko did not seem inclined to throw them out. Even Odo seemed more sympathetic than usual when he saw Nog reunited with his family.

"Come on, Odo," Sisko said, "let's walk the station."

"Yes, sir," Odo said and left with the commander.

Jake and Nog sat on the steps that led up to the commander's office along with Garak, Quark, and Rom. Jake ran his finger across the step he was sitting on and it came away glimmering with golden Keithorpheum dust.

"Is there a Rule of Acquisition that applies here?" Nog asked.

"Yes," Quark said. "The quality of life aboard the station is better with the lights on!" He gave Nog's ear a single sharp tug.

After what seemed to be a long time—yet, for Jake's money, not long enough—O'Brien touched his communication badge. "O'Brien to Sisko."

"Sisko here."

"We're ready, Commander."

"Things are all secure down here," Sisko said. "We'll be right up. Sisko out."

A few minutes later, his father and Odo rose aboard the lift. Sisko went to the steps and stood near Jake. Jake reached up and put his hand into his father's. He wasn't ashamed to admit he was afraid.

"Begin when ready, Chief," Sisko said.

O'Brien pushed a few buttons and suddenly the lights went out. Near him, Nog squeaked softly.

Jake floated free of the step he'd been sitting on—he no longer weighed anything. Weightlessness was not so bad except that his stomach had a nervous, floaty feeling. He swallowed and hung on tight to his father's hand.

Jake had never experienced such absolute darkness. There were no situation lights, no clock faces, no instruments. Not having any light to work with, his eyes produced images of their own—flashing ghost lights, things shimmering just outside his range of vision.

Down on the Promenade they would have starshine coming in through the big windows. He tried to imagine whether the hot points of light would somehow make the darkness seem even more intense.

The silence was not as thick as the darkness, yet it was unusual and frightening. There was no sound of air recirculators, none of the thousands of electronic beeps and boops that normally filled his day from morning till night without him thinking about them

once. The emptiness made a pressure against his ears. He found that he could hear Dax—or was it Kira?—tapping fingers on a console. He could hear himself breathing and the breathing of others. He imagined he could hear his heart beating.

"O'Brien," Sisko called. His voice sounded very loud. It echoed in the big bell of Ops in a way that Jake had never noticed before.

"Sir?" O'Brien said. His voice sounded loud too. Loud and close.

"Let there be light."

"Aye, sir."

A second later Jake fell a few inches to the step he had been floating above. His stomach went back where it belonged. Light and noise filled the room, filled the station. Everyone was sitting or standing exactly where they had been. Sisko gripped Jake's hand tightly, then slowly pulled away. Everything looked so normal Jake could hardly believe that anything had ever been different or wrong. He ran his finger across the step and it came up clean. The Keithorpheum dust was gone.

"How are we doing, Major?" Sisko asked.

Kira was at her situation table. She smiled. "Power availability fifty-five percent and rising." As she spoke, the lights became brighter, the gravity firmer, the sound of the air recirculators more assured. "Sixty-two, seventy-five, eighty-seven . . . ninety-eight percent and holding."

"Ninety-eight percent," O'Brien commented. "Not bad for this old Cardassian tub."

"I want you to run diagnostics on every system on the station," Sisko said. "I want to make sure everything is functioning properly."

Kira, Dax, and O'Brien went to work.

Quark and Rom escorted Nog to the lift. "See you, Jake," Nog called out before they sank out of sight.

"Thank you for believing in me," Garak said as he approached Commander Sisko.

"Oh, I don't believe in you," Sisko said. "I just think we all got lucky this time."

"Surely, you don't think—"

"Major," Sisko called while still glaring at Garak, "do long-range sensors detect any Cardassian ships?"

"No, sir," Kira said.

"What can I say?" Garak asked as he opened his arms and smiled.

"Say that next time you make a suggestion to my son, you'll make damned sure it doesn't endanger the station."

"I promise. Anything else?"

Sisko shook his head. "You must have a shop to tend to."

"Of course," Garak said after studying Sisko for a moment.

Jake followed his father up the stairs and into his office. Sisko found his baseball on the floor and tossed it to Jake. Jake caught it and smiled.

"I'm proud of you, Jake," Sisko said.

"Proud? I thought I was going to get yelled at. This

business with the Nimijks and at least half the trouble with the Keithorpheum was my fault."

"Yours and Nog's."

"Yes."

Sisko sat down behind his desk, and Jake tossed the ball back to him. "We had trouble, it's true," Sisko said as he set the baseball carefully on its stand. "But I like the fact that you admitted your mistakes and took responsibility for your conduct."

"You do?" Jake asked, astonished by his good fortune.

"And the fact that for a kid who claims he's not a technical whiz, you did a good job helping us figure out a course of action."

"Kind of like an adult, huh, Dad?"

"Kind of," Sisko admitted. "I ask only that next time you and Nog have an urge to explore the station, you come to me first. Maybe with my help you can satisfy your curiosity and avoid disasters too."

"Thanks, Dad. I will." He thought for a moment, and then asked a question that had been bothering him. "Do you think Garak knew we'd find that Nimijk figure?"

"The truth is, Jake, I don't know."

"Me neither. But he and the Trulgovians don't seem to be connected, and the Cardassians aren't attacking."

"Not this time, anyway," Sisko agreed. "You find Garak easy to like, don't you?"

"Yeah. Is that okay?"

"So far. Even Garak is innocent until proven guilty. Just do everyone a favor and think twice before you follow his suggestions again."

Jake nodded. He saw an opportunity and he took it. "Um, Dad?"

"Yes, Jake."

"Now that I'm acting kind of like an adult, can I go play the 'K'lshi: Klingon House of Terror' program in a holosuite?"

Jake thought he saw his father smile. But if it happened at all, the smile came and went so quickly that Jake could not be sure.

"No," Commander Sisko said.

Join the STAR TREK™ Fan Club

For only $19.95 you can join **Paramount Pictures' Official** *Star Trek* **Fan Club!** Membership to this exclusive organization includes:

- **A one-year subscription** to the bimonthly *Star Trek Communicator* magazine packed with *Star Trek* photos, interviews and articles! Plus a merchandise insert filled with the latest and greatest *Star Trek* collectibles.

- Membership kit which includes an exclusive set of **Skybox Trading Cards, exclusive collectors' poster, and more!**

- **Discounts** on *Star Trek* merchandise!

- Opportunity to purchase exclusive ***Star Trek* collectibles** available to members only!

Yes! I want to join The Official *Star Trek* Fan Club!
Membership for one-year - $19.95 (Canadian $22.95-U.S. Dollars)
☐ To join by VISA/MasterCard only call 1-800-TRUE-FAN (1-800-878-3326)
☐ I've enclosed my check or money order for $19.95
Name _____
Address _____
City/State _____ Zip _____
Send to:
The Official *Star Trek* Fan Club, P.O. Box 55841, Boulder, CO 80322-5841

TM, ® & © 1996 Paramount Pictures. All Rights Reserved.

1251

STAR TREK®
STARFLEET ACADEMY®

The first adventures of cadets James T. Kirk, Leonard McCoy and the Vulcan Spock!

From Spock's momentous decision to attend Starfleet Academy on Earth, through his first meeting with the medical student McCoy and their action-packed adventure with the ultra-serious, ultra-daring Cadet Kirk, these adventures will take readers "where no one has gone before"™—back to the very beginning!

1 CRISIS ON VULCAN 00078-0/$3.99
By Brad and Barbara Strickland

2 AFTERSHOCK 00079-9/$3.99
By John Vornholt

3 CADET KIRK 00077-2/$3.99
By Diane Carey

A MINSTREL® BOOK
Published by Pocket Books

Simon & Schuster Mail Order Dept. BWB
200 Old Tappan Rd., Old Tappan, N.J. 07675

Please send me the books I have checked above. I am enclosing $_____(please add $0.75 to cover the postage and handling for each order. Please add appropriate sales tax). Send check or money order--no cash or C.O.D.'s please. Allow up to six weeks for delivery. For purchase over $10.00 you may use VISA: card number, expiration date and customer signature must be included.

Name _____

Address _____

City _____ State/Zip _____

VISA Card # _____ Exp.Date _____

Signature _____ 1210-01

TM, ® & © 1996 Paramount Pictures. All Rights Reserved.

THE HARDY BOYS® SERIES By Franklin W. Dixon

☐ #59: NIGHT OF THE WEREWOLF	70993-3/$3.99	
☐ #60: MYSTERY OF THE SAMURAI		
SWORD	67302-5/$3.99	
☐ #61: THE PENTAGON SPY	67221-5/$3.99	
☐ #64: MYSTERY OF SMUGGLERS COVE	66229-5/$3.50	
☐ #69: THE FOUR-HEADED DRAGON	65797-6/$3.50	
☐ #71: TRACK OF THE ZOMBIE	62623-X/$3.50	
☐ #72: THE VOODOO PLOT	64287-1/$3.99	
☐ #75: TRAPPED AT SEA	64290-1/$3.50	
☐ #86: THE MYSTERY OF THE		
SILVER STAR	64374-6/$3.50	
☐ #87: PROGRAM FOR DESTRUCTION	64895-0/$3.99	
☐ #88: TRICKY BUSINESS	64973-6/$3.99	
☐ #89: THE SKY BLUE FRAME	64974-4/$3.99	
☐ #90: DANGER ON THE DIAMOND	63425-9/$3.99	
☐ #91: SHIELD OF FEAR	66308-9/$3.99	
☐ #92: THE SHADOW KILLERS	66309-7/$3.99	
☐ #93: SERPENT'S TOOTH MYSTERY	66310-0/$3.99	
☐ #95: DANGER ON THE AIR	66305-4/$3.50	
☐ #96: WIPEOUT	66306-2/$3.99	
☐ #97: CAST OF CRIMINALS	66307-0/$3.50	
☐ #98: SPARK OF SUSPICION	66304-6/$3.99	
☐ #101: MONEY HUNT	69451-0/$3.99	
☐ #102: TERMINAL SHOCK	69288-7/$3.99	
☐ #103: THE MILLION-DOLLAR		
NIGHTMARE	69272-0/$3.99	
☐ #104: TRICKS OF THE TRADE	69273-9/$3.99	
☐ #105: THE SMOKE SCREEN		
MYSTERY	69274-7/$3.99	
☐ #106: ATTACK OF THE		
VIDEO VILLIANS	69275-5/$3.99	
☐ #107: PANIC ON GULL ISLAND	69276-3/$3.99	
☐ #110: THE SECRET OF SIGMA SEVEN	72717-6/$3.99	
☐ #112: THE DEMOLITION MISSION	73058-4/$3.99	
☐ #113: RADICAL MOVES	73060-6/$3.99	

☐ #114: THE CASE OF THE		
COUNTERFEIT CRIMINALS	73061-4/$3.99	
☐ #115: SABOTAGE AT SPORTS CITY	73062-2/$3.99	
☐ #116: ROCK 'N' ROLL RENEGADES	73063-0/$3.99	
☐ #117: THE BASEBALL CARD CONSPIRACY	73064-9/$3.99	
☐ #118: DANGER IN THE FOURTH DIMENSION	79308-X/$3.99	
☐ #119: TROUBLE AT COYOTE CANYON	79309-8/$3.99	
☐ #120: CASE OF THE COSMIC KIDNAPPING	79310-1/$3.99	
☐ #121: MYSTERY IN THE OLD MINE	79311-X/$3.99	
☐ #122: CARNIVAL OF CRIME	79312-8/$3.99	
☐ #123: ROBOT'S REVENGE	79313-6/$3.99	
☐ #124: MYSTERY WITH A DANGEROUS		
BEAT	79314-4/$3.99	
☐ #125: MYSTERY ON MAKATUNK ISLAND	79315-2/$3.99	
☐ #126: RACING TO DISASTER	87210-9/$3.99	
☐ #127: REEL THRILLS	87211-7/$3.99	
☐ #128: DAY OF THE DINOSAUR	87212-5/$3.99	
☐ #129: THE TREASURE AT DOLPHIN BAY	87213-3/$3.99	
☐ #130: SIDETRACKED TO DANGER	87214-1/$3.99	
☐ #131: CRUSADE OF THE FLAMING SWORD	87215-X/$3.99	
☐ #132: MAXIMUM CHALLENGE	87216-8/$3.99	
☐ #133: CRIME IN THE KENNEL	87217-6/$3.99	
☐ #134: CROSS-COUNTRY CRIME	50517-3/$3.99	
☐ #135: THE HYPERSONIC SECRET	50518-1/$3.99	
☐ #136: THE COLD CASH CAPER	50520-3/$3.99	
☐ #137: HIGH-SPEED SHOWDOWN	50521-1/$3.99	
☐ #138: THE ALASKAN ADVENTURE	50524-6/$3.99	
☐ #139: THE SEARCH FOR THE SNOW LEOPARD	50525-4/$3.99	
☐ #140: SLAM DUNK SABOTAGE	50526-2/$3.99	
☐ #141: THE DESERT THIEVES	50527-0/$3.99	
☐ #142: LOST IN GATOR SWAMP	00054-3/$3.99	
☐ THE HARDY BOYS GHOST STORIES	69133-3/$3.99	

LOOK FOR AN EXCITING NEW
HARDY BOYS MYSTERY COMING FROM
MINSTREL® BOOKS

Simon & Schuster, Mail Order Dept. HB5, 200 Old Tappan Rd., Old Tappan, N.J. 07675

Please send me copies of the books checked. Please add appropriate local sales tax.
☐ Enclosed full amount per copy with this coupon (Send check or money order only)
☐ If order is $10.00 or more, you may charge to one of the following accounts: ☐ Mastercard   ☐ Visa
Please be sure to include proper postage and handling: 0.95 for first copy; 0.50 for each additional copy ordered.

Name _____

Address _____

City _____ State/Zip _____

Books listed are also available at your bookstore. Prices are subject to change without notice.   657-22

#1: THE TALE OF THE SINISTER STATUES
by **John Peel** 52545-X/$3.99
#2: THE TALE OF CUTTER'S TREASURE
by **David L. Seidman** 52729-0/$3.99
#3: THE TALE OF THE RESTLESS HOUSE
by **John Peel** 52547-6/$3.99
#4: THE TALE OF THE NIGHTLY NEIGHBORS
by **D.J. MacHale and Kathleen Derby** 53445-9/$3.99
#5: THE TALE OF THE SECRET MIRROR
by **Brad and Barbara Strickland** 53671-0/$3.99
#6: THE TALE OF THE PHANTOM SCHOOL BUS
by **Brad and Barbara Strickland** 53672-9/$3.99
#7: THE TALE OF THE GHOST RIDERS
by **John Vornholt** 56252-5/$3.99
#8: THE TALE OF THE DEADLY DIARY
by **Brad and Barbara Strickland** 53673-7/$3.99
#9: THE TALE OF THE VIRTUAL NIGHTMARE
by **Ted Pedersen** 00080-2/$3.99
#10: THE TALE OF THE CURIOUS CAT
by **Diana G. Gallagher** 00081-0/$3.99
#11: THE TALE OF THE ZERO HERO
by **John Peel** 00357-7/$3.99

A MINSTREL® BOOK

Simon & Schuster Mail Order Dept. BWB
200 Old Tappan Rd., Old Tappan, N.J. 07675

Please send me the books I have checked above. I am enclosing $_____(please add $0.75 to cover the
postage and handling for each order. Please add appropriate sales tax). Send check or money order--no cash
or C.O.D.'s please. Allow up to six weeks for delivery. For purchase over $10.00 you may use VISA: card
number, expiration date and customer signature must be included.

Name _____

Address _____

City _____ State/Zip _____

VISA Card # _____ Exp.Date _____

Signature _____ 1053-11